A Hint of Romance
Collection of Short Stories by

Pamela S Thibodeaux

"I have found the one whom my soul loves."
~ Song of Solomon 3:4 (NASB)

A Hint of Romance
Collection of Short Stories
by
Pamela S Thibodeaux

Publisher/Distributor:
Temperance Publishing; an imprint of
Pamela S. Thibodeaux Enterprises, LLC
PO Box 324
Iowa, LA 70647

ISBN: 979-8-9895650-2-3

Cover Design: GetCovers.com

Publishing History: *The Big Catch, Review of Love, In His Sight* and *A Hero for Jessica* were previously published individually **and** in *Love in Season* anthology through Pelican Book Group 2007-2020   *All Rights have Reverted to Author*

All scripture quotations, unless otherwise indicated, are taken from the Holy Bible, New International Version(R), NIV(R), Copyright 1973, 1978, 1984, 2011 by Biblica, Inc.™ Used by permission of Zondervan. All rights reserved worldwide. www.zondervan.com

Note:
This collection is a work of fiction. Names, characters, places, and incidents are either the product of the author's imagination, or, if real, used fictitiously.

Contents

Dedication

For Karla: *family by blood, sisters of the heart, friends forever ~*

You left us too soon.
I love and miss you.
(B/F/C/S/A)

Thank You...

If you've been a friend/fan of my work for long, you may recognize some of these stories from previous publications–either through Pelican Book Group or limited editions offered exclusively to my newsletter audience. Do not worry that you're paying for reprints of stuff you've already bought and/or read!

A few have never been published in any way, shape, or form.

Either way, I pray you are as blessed as I am by your purchase of this book. If you enjoy **A Hint of Romance,** please write a positive review, and post it at online retailers and websites where readers gather and/or your social media platforms (FaceBook, Good Reads, BookBub, Twitter, etc). If you haven't already, sign up to receive my **Newsletter** and get a FREE short story.

Twin Flames

Ray grabbed the phone before it rang a third time. "Double R Ranch. May I help you?"

"Mr. or Ms. MacFarland, please."

The scent of honeyed whiskey filled his mind at the throaty voice. Tingles raced up his spine. "This is Ray."

"I'm Cheyanne Williams, I'd like to speak with you about the office manager position you have available."

Ray pulled the chair out from under the desk and sank into it. Never before had the mere sound of a woman's voice scattered his composure. He cleared his throat. "Do you have a resume?"

"Yes, but I'm out of town right now. May I email it to you?"

"Sure." Ray rattled off his email address and promised to get back with her, then hung up the phone. Excitement raced over him. He sure hoped this last detail would be resolved before they opened for business.

From the moment he and his twin sister inherited their great uncle's home and conceived the idea of turning the small ranch into a guest venue complete with horseback rides, hiking trails, campfires and hayrides, everything had fallen into place. Ray loved it when life showed up in a grand way and all of his plans came together with such precision.

The computer jingled, signaling incoming mail.

Ray opened the email and attachment. He barely had time to skim the resume when the phone rang again. "Double R Ranch."

"Cheyanne Williams again, just making sure you received my resume."

"Yes, and I'd like to schedule an interview."

"As I mentioned, I'm out of town and will be for several days. Can we Skype perhaps?"

Nerves knotted his stomach at the thought. Ray hated anything resembling a camera, had to all but be drawn and quartered to take a picture with his sister for their website. Barely able to operate the basics of a computer, there's no chance in hell he'd try to tackle an electronic face-to-face program. "How about we just see you when you get back?"

"Great! I'll be in touch."

A week of conflicting schedules, a dozen emails, and half as many conversations later, they were once again trying to plan a face-to-face consultation.

"It's difficult to make a firm decision without meeting you, but your resume and our conversations lead me to believe you're the best candidate. Since you haven't mentioned salary requirements, my only concern is that we won't be able to pay you what you're worth." Ray held his breath and waited for her response. A soft laugh rumbled over the line and sent a delicious tingle along every nerve in his body.

"I have an Associate's Degree and a hundred years' experience working in every type of business known to man, none of which have made me completely happy as I feel working at the ranch will, so salary is not an issue. I knew, and adored, the previous owner, and love what you've done to the old place. I would enjoy, be honored in fact, to be a part of this."

"Well, we're having our open house tomorrow. Hopefully you can join us."

"Count on it. I look forward to meeting you in person."

Ray placed both hands on the desk, palms down and fingers wide, and took deep breaths to restore his inner calm. Thick and rich, the southern inflection to the silky timbre filled him with warmth he hadn't felt in years. *If ever.*

"Who was that?" his sister asked from the doorway.

Ray inhaled sharply and tried to direct his scrambled thoughts into some semblance of order. "Cheyanne Williams. She's coming to the open house tomorrow night."

Raelee arched a brow at him. "The office

manager with the sexy voice?"

Ray nodded. "Crazy, right?"

"Au contraire. Pretty cool if you ask me, and about time you started feeling again."

"Don't go there, Raelee."

"It's true! Ever since *your* wife ran off with *my* husband, you've beaten yourself up feeling guilty one minute and relieved the next, only to shut down completely until these past couple of years."

"Which is why I'm grateful you decided to do this with me," Ray remarked. "Turning Great-Uncle Alfred's old homestead into a guest ranch has been good for both of us."

"Yes it has. Now that things are settled and we're about to open, maybe we can think about our future."

Ray shrugged. Unlike his sister whose faith and optimism allowed her to bounce back from adversity quite easily, it took years after the end of his brief, disastrous marriage for him to grow from feeling like a blithering idiot into the strong, self-assured man he now considered himself to be. "I've no desire to join the herds of men trolling the bars in search of a woman. If I'm meant to marry again, the perfect *lady* will show up when she's supposed to."

Raelee smirked. "Yeah, but not if she doesn't know where you are."

Ray brushed the familiar arguments away with a wave. "I'll be happy to hire a decent office manager. I'd much rather be in the corral or mucking stalls than taking reservations and dealing with paperwork."

Raelee shuddered. "Me too."

Ray chuckled. His sister had a penchant for overspending and couldn't balance a check book to save her life, but her culinary and people skills made her the perfect partner for this venture. "You'll have plenty to do with the cooking, cleaning and socializing."

She slipped her arm through his with a wink and grin. "Who knows, I might meet a tall, dark and handsome cowboy after all."

He shook his head with a snicker. "Your lifelong fantasy?"

She snorted in a very unladylike manner. "Beats a stiff-necked businessman like the sleaze ball I trusted and married ten years ago. Those two deserve each other and every bit of misery they conjure up together."

He loved her fierce loyalty, the unique way she handled anything life threw her way, and her firm belief in karma. "You're right and we'll leave them to it."

****

The next evening Ray waited for his sister in their suite of rooms on the third floor of the old Colonial style home. The open house was scheduled to begin in less than an hour. Pride stole his breath when she stepped out of her room to stand beside him in front of the large, ornate mirror in the sitting area. From the moment of birth, no one could mistake them as twins.

Both had the same course, curly hair–although Raelee had tamed hers into a stream of dark silk that flirted with her waist–finely chiseled features, and expressive gray eyes. Raymond and Raelee MacFarland had always been a pair to contend with no matter what they set their minds to. He hoped this venture would be no different.

He offered her his arm. "Every cowboy who walks through our door is toast."

Raelee laughed and hugged him. "Same true of every woman. Remember when we used to plan on marrying twins?"

He chortled. "Yeah. Guess we missed out on that one."

She giggled, slid her hand through the crook of his elbow. "You never know what the future holds."

The two of them walked downstairs moments before people began to gather and mingle.

The cowbell on the front door jangled followed by a husky laugh that caused Ray's heart to stumble while his pulse sprinted into a gallop. He watched as the auburn-haired beauty stepped through the entrance; her head tilted toward her escort. His sister's sharp inhale and murmured, "oh my," had him taking a closer look as the two zeroed in on them.

"Mr. MacFarland?" He'd recognize that voice anywhere. It feathered over him like a caress. Ray nodded and reached for her proffered hand with a smile.

"I'm Cheyanne Williams. This is my brother Shane. We thought you might need another wrangler."

No mistaking they were twins also.

Her eyes glowed like polished emeralds; hand felt like satin in his. Ray's heart did a slow waltz into his stomach. He noted Shane's blatant interest in Raelee and the smitten look on her face and slid his sister a wink. "We just might at that."

Dear Reader,

Like Ray and his sister, we've all experienced disappointment in our lives. Though hopefully nothing like theirs LOL! But, like Raelee if we choose faith and optimism instead of fear and pessimism, God will work all things together for our good.

It's a promise. (see Romans 8:28)

If you don't know HIM already, I pray you will seek a personal relationship with God, the Creator of our Universe and the Lord, Jesus Christ. If you do, I pray you'll continue to draw closer to Him and in all things you will give Him praise.

The Big Catch

"You have to jerk harder than that," Jeffrey chided, unable to disguise the hint of amusement in his voice.

I held my breath and counted to twenty. The last time he corrected me, I'd jerked *too hard.* ix Six months into what I thought was the love of my life, we'd discovered some uncommon ground. Namely, The Great Outdoors.

Oh, I loved swimming, hiking, tennis, ball games, all manner of sports. Blue skies, warm water, all of God's earth was glorious. Especially in summertime.

Jeffrey had other ideas of how to enjoy the beauty of nature. Fishing. Red fish, snapper, flounder, speckled trout, bass, catfish, white perch. Anything that came off a hook, fresh from a canal, pond, lake, or river. Fresh water, salt water, it didn't matter as long as he could be out there fishing.

For the life of me, I couldn't figure it out. What—exactly—could anyone get out of putting an innocent little fish on a hook to attract a bigger one? I mean, luring that poor, unsuspecting fish to its death while causing the death of another. And catch and release? That was a plain old waste of time. Why spend all that effort and energy catching a fish only to turn it loose? Then, there were the hours spent away from land or any form of civilization. In a boat, in the middle of nowhere, with only the heat and insects to contend with, not to mention Mother Nature's mercurial temperament.

The whole concept was beyond me. Baked, broiled, or fried, was the limit to my understanding of fish. However, after months of coaxing, urging, and downright begging, I agreed to give it a try. Now, barely two hours after leaving dry land, I'd about had it. My maiden voyage was turning out to be a disaster. I was either jerking too hard or not hard enough. My line spent more time out of than *in* the water, usually caught on some buried treasure hidden deep below the surface or in a tangled mess from my inept casting abilities.

For some unknown reason, the art, beauty, and challenge of catching a fish eluded me. Still, I had to hand it to him; Jeffrey was a study in patience.

Tossing my line over to him once more, I shuddered in disgust as he stuck the hook through the head of a squirming minnow and baited my line for the umpteenth time. Tossing it into the murky water, I prayed for luck *or a sudden rainstorm.*

"Watch him Karla," Jeff said, as the cork on my line began to bob and twitch. "Easy, now.

Wait." Quietly and gently, he guided me in watching and waiting for the right moment to set the hook.

I was more interested in the sound of his voice than what was going on with my line. Jeff always sounded as though he'd just rolled out of bed. Thick, husky, and warm, his voice alone could seduce me into a puddle.

"Now!"

The sudden command startled me, and I jerked with all my might. Jeff's guffaw rent the air, and I had to force myself not to hit him with the rod.

"You jerked his lips off." His brown eyes danced with humor.

"That's not funny. You startled me. It's your fault I jerked too hard." A pout stretched my lips.

"I'm not laughing at you, sweetheart. I'm laughing with you," he insisted, nearly doubled over with mirth.

"Right." I fought the urge to throw the fishing contraption–hook, line, and sinker–into the lake.

"Aw, c'mon now. Chin up. You'll always be my favorite fishing partner."

Silky, smooth, and seductive, his voice turned my insides to mush.

"Don't worry, you'll get it right next time.

Practice makes perfect you know."

There won't be a next time, I thought, but bit back the retort.

As the sun rose higher and the morning grew hotter, my patience got shorter. I decided to take a break while Jeff untangled and repaired my line yet again. Putting away my rod and reel, as per his instructions, I stretched back in my seat. The trolling motor purred as Jeffrey worked the bank. The tension dissipated, and I began to relax.

My fingers trailed in the cool, salty water as we moved idly along. Waves lapping against the boat combined with its gentle rocking lulled my soul into a quiet, peaceful state. Seagulls dove greedily into schools of baitfish or shrimp and came up with a screech of triumph or disappointment.

Large, gray-tinged clouds floated on a soft breeze across an otherwise clear sky, providing a bit of shelter from the rising sun. There was an angel and a mouse. All around, nature was a symphony of sight and sound.

Now this, I could get used to—nature in all her glory and Jeff in his. Watching him was like poetry in motion.

I retrieved the suntan oil from the tackle box and smoothed it on every inch of exposed skin. Tucking my hair under the wide-brimmed, straw hat I wore, I adjusted my sunglasses and enjoyed seeing him in action. His broad shoulders flexed and rippled with every cast. His excitement was contagious. I got a kick out of his smile and triumphant little snicker every time he caught a keeper, and the way he'd joke and pretend to kiss the ones he threw back.

How he could concentrate on so many things at once—fishing, working the trolling motor, carrying on a conversation—and never miss a bite, never lose his train of thought, was amazing. He glanced at me, winked, and the frustrations of the morning faded away like the last, lingering, wisps of morning fog.

The sun sat nearly straight up in the sky before Jeff was ready to take a break. Stacking the rods neatly in their rack, he helped me trade places with him. His lips lowered toward mine.

"Whoa, boy, these ain't no fish lips." Considering the morning I'd endured, I couldn't help but take a turn teasing him.

His answering chuckle was soft, throaty. "Oh, no, sugar lips," he murmured in that beautiful voice. I melted. After a quick brush of his mouth across mine, Jeff started the motor, and we sped off to a quiet, secluded cove.

Lunch was dry bologna sandwiches, soggy chips, gooey cookies, and ice-cold colas. Sharing it with Jeffrey made my romantic heart think of a candlelight dinner at a secluded table for two in a fancy restaurant. The bright, noonday, sun took on a soft, intimate, glow. His tender teasing, gentle laughter, and sweet kisses made me glad I'd come along, but not overly anxious to try my hand at fishing again.

A quiet, uninterrupted, lunch and then we were back at it. Though not as disastrous, the afternoon wasn't much more successful than the morning. For me anyway. I barely got the hang of casting my line without causing it to backlash before it was time to leave. By the time we picked up the boat and headed home, the sun was well into its descent, and I was exhausted. The day hadn't been a total waste. Jeff caught a stringer full. I caught sunburn.

Though I sported a healthy tan all year, the difference in normal exposure to the summer sun, compared with its glare off saltwater, even with SPF protection, turned my skin into an angry red mass and forced me to take a few days of sick leave from my job.

Bright and early Monday morning, a rose appeared on my doorstep. *A rose for a rose*, the card read. All that week, Jeff showered me with trinkets, and gifts, lavishing me with affection to show his appreciation for my sportsmanship and to apologize for my discomfort. Every evening, he came over and rubbed the ointment prescribed by my doctor into my parched, dry skin, soothing it, and me, and then followed up with gentle kisses.

As my skin healed, I began to look at fishing in a different light. Though I hadn't caught more than rays, I had enjoyed the beauty of nature with the man I loved. Still, I begged off for the next few weekends.

My next fishing trip wasn't as disastrous, or as long. Simply a quiet morning spent in the boat with Jeff. The small saltwater lake fed off the Gulf of Mexico providing a variety of treasures and even I was able to catch a few speckled trout. We shared lunch on a blanket on the ground beneath a huge oak tree at a roadside park. That evening we watched a romantic movie, sharing popcorn, peanuts, and colas.

As the summer dwindled into early fall, the colors of nature turned to beautiful shades of red and gold. The days were cooler. The nights, longer. My fishing technique improved. On the one-year anniversary of our first date, Jeff proposed.

We'd gone out on the boat that morning. Jeff fished. I sat back in my seat and watched him. Enjoying our time together. Breathing in the crisp fall air, and the beauty of nature all around. Sights, sounds, and smells that I'd come to appreciate. That evening we shared a candlelight dinner and wine at the Starlight Bar and Grill, the same place we'd had dinner exactly one year ago. Jeff told me again that I was his favorite fishing partner. Then, with a tender smile and a kiss, he gave me a gift.

Skillfully sculpted in wood and beautifully hand-painted, was a carving of a man in a boat. You could almost feel the gentle lap of the white-tipped waves against the bow. The guy looked a little like Jeff—warm golden skin, and that special smile. From the tiny tackle box opened to display an array of lures to the stringer of fish hanging off the side of the boat, every detail was intricately carved and painstakingly complete.

The artist had even captured that sparkle in a fisherman's eye when he caught a big one.

At the end of a tiny rod and reel, sporting real fishing line, was a ring. A petite heart-shaped diamond set in a brilliant gold band. Gazing into my eyes Jeff asked if I'd be his partner for life. Without hesitating I said yes.

After only a few fishing trips, looks like I'd caught myself a keeper.

Dear Reader,

How often are we like Karla, reluctant to try new things or hesitant to step out of our comfort zone because we don't understand the whys and wherefores of someone else's passion or don't know how to do something? Even if we don't enjoy the same activities, there is pleasure to be found by simply being in the presence of those we love.

Next time your significant other invites you to tag along while he or she does their thing, I urge you to put aside your reasons why you can't go and grasp the opportunity to simply be together. Then *listen* when he or she talks about their passion. Feel his or her enthusiasm and bask in the pleasure of spending quality time in each other's company.

After all, relationships are built (or broken) on communication and compromise.

Something to think about....

Like a Rock

"I won't leave if you don't."

As usual the humor in my husband's voice and love in his eyes lifted my spirits. I smiled at him. "I'm not going anywhere."

At home, our youngest daughter packed her car for college while my husband and I drove the oldest child to the airport. Her flight back to the Air base soared above us.

Jerry took my hand in his, grinned over at me. "What'll we do now, Macey, with no kids in the house?"

All the plans we'd made over the years frolicked like fairy dust in the air... Dancing the night away. Long walks on the beach. Sleeping late. Trips within the continental United States and abroad.

Mountains and shorelines, hiking and canoeing—the future spread out before us, bright with hope and possibilities. We'd dreamt, planned, and invested to ensure we'd be able to do all the things we wanted, when this time in our lives arrived.

So why did I feel so down? Was this normal for empty nesters?

Jerry lifted my hand to his mouth, brushed his lips over my knuckles. "I'm thinking we should go camping this weekend and celebrate."

The ache in my chest felt as though tiny shards of shattered glass were being embedded one-by-one into my heart. I took a deep breath and massaged the area. "Celebrate?"

His expression sent my pulse into a tailspin.

"Yeah, you know, like newlyweds or something."

The suggestion sparked emotions between us we hadn't explored in quite some time. My stomach clenched like a nervous fist. "Where would we go on such short notice?"

He shrugged. "Doesn't matter, we'll pack up and head out toward our favorite spots. We're sure to find a site somewhere."

The next morning, we packed the RV with a week's supply of summer clothing and food and left with nothing more than a list of places to visit. No plan. No reservations. Just off on a new escapade.

As Jerry drove, I called ahead until I had several possible camp sites for the night. Choosing one we hadn't visited in a while, I programmed the destination into the GPS, and settled in with a book I'd wanted to read for months.

The story grabbed me by the throat, drew me in. Before long I was engrossed in a modern tale of four friends who'd found themselves alone, one way or another, once their children had flown the nest. Less than halfway through the novel, I slammed it shut. "Stupid."

Jerry glanced over his eyebrow arched in question.

I shoved the volume into my bag, flicked away a tear, then turned the radio to a rock and roll oldies station. *I will not ruin our trip by a phobia I didn't know existed until that silly book.*

Still the questions nagged at me. Would those women make it through the changes in their lives?

Would we?

Six hours and two pit-stops later, we pulled into an RV park and finished setting up the camper as the sun began its descent.

Jerry took my hand. "Let's take a walk."

A walk with my husband was always an adventure. Several times he twirled me into a waltz, humming our favorite song. Other times, he wandered off to collect pretty stones or pick wildflowers. Twining the stems together, he handed me a bouquet as we reached a spot where heaven and earth met in a glorious profusion of rock and sky.

Colors bled from the clouds and onto the hills in various shades of peach, gold and purple. We gazed over the landscape to where the dusky orange orb sank below twin peaks and cast shadows in the shape of a heart.

Jerry wrapped his arms around my waist, pulled me back against his chest, and rested his cheek against mine.

"See that rock?" He pointed to the mountainous formation east of the heart-shaped peaks.

Too overwhelmed by the beauty before me to speak, I nodded.

"My love is like that rock. It's strong, solid, and well able to weather the storms of life. It'll never change. It'll last forever, and there's not another one like it in the world."

I turned in his arms and placed my palm against his cheek as his lips lowered to mine in a sweet embrace. Without a word or even a hint of my unexpected fears, I received the reassurance I needed from the man I'd loved since high school.

The End

Dear Reader,

Many of you have heard the story of how, early in our courtship, my beloved Terry gave me a rock and said… "My love is like this rock. It's strong and solid, it'll never change, it'll last forever, and there's not another one like it in the world."

That has stayed with me throughout the years and comforted me at the oddest times since his death in 2009.

If you have a loved one, please tell them often how you feel and understand that the little things you do for one another will stay with them forever. Therefore, follow your impulse and do something sweet, silly, or special, because you never know what the lasting impact may be.

If you don't know HIM already, I pray you will seek a personal relationship with the Lord, Jesus Christ and if you do, that you'll continue to draw closer to Him and in all things you will give Him praise.

A Hero for Jessica

Anthony Paul Seville prepared for the evening ahead. Impeccably groomed, his Oscar de la Renta suit was the height of fashion–dark gray with lighter pinstripes that he'd been told brought to life the silver in his hair and the glint in his eyes.

As a lawyer and professor, he found the upcoming event to be confining. Still, he'd promised. This was the first, and only, time he'd ever agreed to host a lecture on the finer points of the law. On a Friday no less.

With a weary sigh, he walked out of his Penthouse apartment in Jackson Square and made his way to the parking garage that housed his BMW convertible. Within moments, he arrived at the New Orleans Hilton, and entered the conference room where he would host the small, informal lecture.

Early as planned, he walked around and familiarized himself with the seating arrangements. The *reserved* cards, which bore the names of people who would attend, were filed in his memory as quickly and effectively as facts surrounding an important case would be. He sensed more than heard a movement at the door, and turned to greet Mr. Philip Monroe, Dean of Loyola University.

"Hi Phil." Paul stretched out a hand and let a huge grin split his face. He felt the older man wince and loosened his grip, knowing that arthritis had reduced Phil's handshake to a mere version of his earlier days. However, both Phil's smile and the light in his eyes reflected admiration and gratitude that he would give up his Friday night to do this favor for a friend.

"Any set plans for the lecture this evening?"

Paul shrugged. "Not really. I've racked my brain all afternoon but I'm not sure exactly what these people want to know. There were no preliminary questionnaires or anything to give me a clue. Thought I'd just leave the floor open for discussion and answer the questions that come up. What do you think?"

"Sounds like a plan to me. And, Paul, I appreciate this. I really do. It's great publicity for the profession. Not to mention the university."

Paul tossed away the gratitude with a shrug. "No problem Phil, none at all."

They turned in unison as a young woman stumbled into the room. Her eyes widened as the heel of her shoe caught in her dress, ripping the hem. Paul lifted an amused brow at the muttered curse that slipped through the beautifully painted lips and the look of mortification that quickly followed.

"May we help you?"

Jessica's head jerked up in surprise at the sound of his voice. *That Southern drawl.* She stood mesmerized, staring at the man she'd sought to meet for so long. Of their own accord her eyes closed. Embarrassment washed over her in angry waves and left her cheeks stinging in its wake.

"Umm." She cleared her throat and hoped her voice sounded stronger than she felt. "I'm here for the lecture."

With an indolent gesture, he glanced at his watch then back at her. "A mite early, aren't you?"

Another rush of heat burned her cheeks. She lifted her chin in defiance but refrained from comment. Mr. Anthony Paul Seville might be one of the best, most-sought-after lawyers in New Orleans, or Louisiana for that matter, but he wasn't going to make her feel like a fool. She managed that quite nicely all by herself, thank you very much.

His stride possessed an elegant, lazy grace when he walked toward her.

"May I escort you to your seat, Miss...?" His brow lifted in question.

"Aucoin. Jessica Aucoin. And, no, thank you. I believe I can find it myself."

He glanced down at the torn hem of her

dress and then back at her face. Amusement lit his midnight gaze and set her teeth on edge.

"Well, Miss Aucoin. It's the desk in front. Last row I believe." He bent to pick up the book satchel she'd dropped while she clung precariously to the doorframe.

"Thank you." Jessica clenched one fist into the folds of her dress, the other around the handle of the satchel, and walked cautiously to the other side of the room. Finding her place, she sat as gracefully as possible with legs that wobbled. Paul Seville's reputed looks and manner were not unknown to her, but nothing, absolutely nothing, could have prepared her for the real thing.

An excited buzz began to fill the room as people arrived and took their seats. After a brief introduction from Mr. Monroe, the lecture began.

Spellbound, Jessica watched while the man handled even the densest of questions with absolute solemnity. As a writer of romantic suspense and mysteries, she'd followed his career for years and fashioned some of her best stories after his most bizarre cases. While she watched, the idea for her latest creation came to life, and she determined he would make a perfect hero.

He wasn't a large man, five-nine or ten and

slight of form, but unbearably handsome. Splashes of silver streaked his hair, belied his age, enhanced the aura of professionalism and authority he exuded, and came across as purely sensual. Passion and intelligence glowed in the midnight eyes. Yes, she decided mentally, Paul Seville would definitely make the perfect hero. *As well as the perfect lawyer to handle the legal battle I'm about to engage in.*

****

The importance of eye contact was ignored as Paul's gaze continually strayed to the young woman seated at the first table in the last row. *Jessica Aucoin.* Somehow the name rang a bell. For the life of him, he could not place her. But her presence was definitely noticed. Raven hair framed a face of heartbreaking beauty.

Classically oval, the high cheekbones were softened by thick lashed, almond-shaped, eyes— a prominent feature in Creole/French women and their descendants. Only hers weren't dark brown or black, but brilliant green and glowed with admiration and interest, though she never uttered the first question.

The lecture came to an end an hour later than scheduled. Relieved, yet oddly bereft, Paul drove home. His mouth twisted into a grim line when he remembered the not-so-subtle offers by some of the women. All with the exception of one, and he wondered where she'd gone. She must have left through the door with the throng of others. He'd watched for her, but somehow she slipped by him.

He knew how women looked at him, that he was known as the most eligible bachelor in New Orleans, the best catch in Louisiana. He was wealthy, powerful, and dynamic.

And he was alone, completely, and explicably alone.

****

Paul arose as usual on Saturday morning at five-thirty and prepared for his daily run. A cup of coffee, a Bible verse, and then he was off.

A heavy mist reached its muggy arms across the Mississippi river and hugged the city. The river had reached an all-time low. The smell of mud and dead fish, mixed with more pleasant aromas filtering from area cafes, assailed his nostrils as Paul jogged along the river walk.

His mind wandered back to the evening before and he, once again, found himself intrigued by the mystery that was Ms. Jessica Aucoin. He mulled the name and image over in his mind, positive he'd seen her before. But where?

Despite his mind being preoccupied, the ingrained habit of running the same path for years had him turning left at the end of the river walk. He passed through a small alley and crossed the street to head back home. It still amazed him how one side of the street passed along the river, quiet and tranquil, while the other usually bustled with people. Not this morning though. Not yet anyway.

The interlude between the night crawlers and the day creatures was his favorite slice of time. There were enough people about to feel secure, yet enough absence of them to be at peace. The place would come alive within a couple of hours as tourists arrived, and souvenir shops opened to hawk their wares.

He glanced at the window of a small, cozy bookstore along his path and stopped. His breath faltered in surprise. The one and only Miss Jessica Aucoin stared out at him from the back of a book cover. He leaned against the store window as facts began to fill his brain: Writer. Romantic suspense. Very sought after. A star on the rise.

Why on earth had she attended a lecture on the basics of law? He glanced at his watch, muttered a curse, and then continued on his way. The bookstore wouldn't open until nine o'clock, no sense in standing around and staring into the window.

He returned to his apartment, retrieved the newspaper out of its box, and went inside. He rinsed the small two-cup coffee maker–which was actually only one good mug–poured water and measured out grounds for his second cup of the day.

While the coffee brewed, he showered and shaved, and then sat down to read his paper. One of the first things to catch his eye was the announcement of a book signing later that afternoon at the bookstore he'd passed, which featured none other than Miss Jessica Aucoin.

Paul didn't believe in coincidence. There was a reason their paths had crossed. He aimed to find out. He finished with the paper and booted up his computer. His coffee grew cold as he searched the Internet for whatever he could find about Miss Aucoin.

What he discovered surprised and intrigued him.

The only daughter of a wealthy Congressman, Jessica hailed from a small town in southern Florida. Though not one to flaunt the fact, she wasn't ashamed of it. Nor did she hesitate to use the connection when necessary. Her talent unmistakable, reviews and interviews that raved she was a star on the rise, were everywhere. But the more he studied, the more convinced he became that Jessica's appearance at the lecture last night must be more than casual interest in the law. Hints of copyright infringement and plagiarism underscored some of the articles and reviews in blatant, highly liable, and all but slanderous, detail.

Two hours later he had no doubt that he'd see Ms. Aucoin again. Always one to take the initiative, he decided to pay her a surprise visit later that afternoon.

****

Not as spacious as what you'd find in the larger conglomerates, the tiny sitting area offered by the bookstore provided a little islet of peace in the midst of the streams of people who wandered in, out and about. A haven of comfort and relaxation. Housing a couple of chairs, matching footstools, a love seat, as well as end and coffee tables, the tiny oasis resembled a comfortable living room instead of coffee shop.

Antique, ornate lamps provided enough light for reading without the harsh glare of florescent bulbs. Much like a library, the atmosphere encouraged silence, or at the very least, whispering, so as not to disturb other readers.

He had come early. Hoping to talk with her before fans poured in for the signing, he'd picked up a few of her books, wandered into the secluded area and chosen a chair that gave him a clear view of the table set up for her.

He saw her arrive, but waited and watched while she flitted about, setting out decorative figurines and arranged photos, books, and other promotional items. From his seat, Paul watched the exchange between Jessica and some tall, fair man.

He noticed her reaction when the man approached. The look of trepidation that crossed her lovely features. The wary expression in her eyes, which was quickly replaced by anger. The hushed fury in her tone, though her voice was slightly above a whisper. *Wonder what's going on here.*

He stepped out from behind the bookshelves which separated them and noticed her expression had changed from fury to fear. He knew he'd gotten her attention when Jessica turned, breathed a sigh, and moved forward to greet him, hand outstretched.

"Mr. Seville. How very nice to see you again."

"The pleasure's all mine." Paul lifted her hand to his lips and watched her visitor through lowered lids.

A dark flush crept up the man's neck. Anger clouded his face. His eyes took on an ominous glow. The guy spun on his heel and stormed off while muttering under his breath.

"Friend of yours?"

"Hardly." Jessica disengaged her hand from his. The icy tone of her voice warned him not to pry.

He supposed now was neither the time nor place for such a discussion. There'd be enough time for that later. He'd make sure of it.

"Would you like me to sign those for you?" She indicated the books under his arm with a pointed look.

He handed her the books without another word, watched, and waited while she stepped over to the table, slid into the chair and searched for a pen. When she didn't find one right away, her beautiful eyes grew watery with unshed tears. No woman would cry over not being able to find a pen. That guy must have truly upset her.

He reached into his pocket and then handed her a pen. Like an electrical conduit, her warmth permeated the slender, gold tube. She smiled her thanks, hurriedly wrote a greeting, and signed her name, then handed him the books.

Paul was not immune to the changes in atmosphere. The icy tension had dissipated, only to be replaced by one of a more intimate nature. He sensed her tremble, noticed her heightened color, and felt the breath back up in his lungs. *The woman was too beautiful for words.*

A tiny, but vital, very vital, step back broke the sensual charge between them. He'd never forget the moment of awareness that sparked between them nor the quick spurt of longing that surged through his system at the sight of her sitting there, those fathomless green eyes swimming with tears, and a wealth of conflicting emotions.

He took the books, read the inscription, mumbled his thanks, and strode to the checkout counter as readers gathered, vying for her attention.

****

At nearly ten o'clock that evening, Jessica realized she still had Paul's pen. Scheduled from two to four o'clock, the book signing had run well past six. A firm believer that no fan goes unnoticed, no book unsigned, and no conversation unattended, she usually stayed as long as the store was open or until the manager ran her off.

By the time she cleared the table, repacked

her things, and stopped for a bite to eat, it was nearly eight o'clock. A horse-drawn carriage ride topped off her evening, and put her spirit to rest, after the long, arduous day.

Now, alone in her hotel room, she allowed herself to experience the gamut of emotions she'd held at bay all afternoon and evening. The rage. The fear. The fire.

Running the pen through her fingers, she could still feel Paul's touch. The firm but gentle grasp of his hand. The shiver of excitement. The heat. She didn't even have to close her eyes to envision him as he'd looked this afternoon. Whether dressed informally or in a suit and tie, the man was gorgeous. But casual worked so much better.

Despite being cropped short his dark hair fell in thick waves across his forehead. The cotton slacks he'd worn conformed to the muscles in his not long, but well-toned legs, and accentuated the pure masculine physique.

Rolled up at the elbows, his plaid shirt had been tucked into the waist of his pants and outlined the firm abdomen and strong chest, while his white T-shirt was a stark contrast against the tanned skin which showed through the open collar.

There was something intimately appealing about him. Strength of character, gentleness of spirit, all wrapped up in a package that would make any woman swoon with longing.

Drawing a tub full of water, she added liberal amounts of bubbles, sank into the scented, frothy liquid, and let her mind wander. Dreams and visions danced in her head until her fingers itched to hit the keyboard, and she had no choice but to write.

****

In bed that night, Paul didn't have time to consider Jessica or the fact that she still had his pen. His favorite gold pen. He was too caught up in conspiracy and espionage. *Twilight Sorcery* wasn't exactly what the title indicated. There were no witches or warlocks, only an extremely crooked cop, an equally brilliant detective, a beautiful woman, and a hint of voodoo that kept him intrigued until he finally fell asleep with the book in his hand.

He awoke Sunday morning, groggy and disoriented from reading so late into the night. He couldn't remember the last time he'd been so caught up in a story that sleep eluded him. Most of the reading he'd done to date was for work or school, rarely for pleasure.

He fumbled with the coffee pot, rinsed it, poured water, measured grounds, turned it on, and then splashed cold water on his face and waited for it to brew. He sat at the table, picked up the sequel, thumbed through it, and skimmed a few random pages to see if it drew him in like the other had. Only the thought of that first cup of coffee prevented his getting too engrossed in the story to put it down.

That Jessica could craft such deep, well-defined characters amazed him. People he identified with on every level.

Not only the good guys either. The villain whispered to his darker side, the brilliant detective, his mind, and the woman—beautiful, sensitive, vulnerable, and intelligent—his inner man. Something about her reminded him of Jessica.

Oh, he'd heard all the rhetoric about how writers poured themselves into their characters, especially those of the same gender. But it was more than that. She pulled at him. Even through her characters, she entranced.

And it wasn't purely physical, though there was plenty of that.

Something about her more than piqued his interest and captivated his imagination; it reached deep inside his heart to his very soul.

Paul shook his head to clear away the befuddled musings, rose and poured himself a much-needed cup of coffee, then sat back down.

Once again, he thumbed through *Inherent Evil* the sequel to *Twilight Sorcery*. Before he could be drawn into the story, the phone rang, and the caller ID screen flashed. Paul answered with a smile. "Hello, Mom."

"Anthony Paul Seville, where have you been? I haven't heard from you in days. Have you been taking care of yourself, eating right, exercising, and getting proper rest? Are you coming over here today? Will you be here for lunch? Are you bringing your laundry?"

Well-rehearsed in the normal tirade, Paul chuckled. Unable to interject a single word, much less answer a question, he waited until she took a breath before he responded to all with one phrase. "Yes, Ma'am."

So much for reading this afternoon.

"You're a good son, Paul." He could hear the smile in her voice.

"Thanks, Mom. I'll be there shortly. But don't cook. I'm taking you out to lunch."

"But what about your laundry?"

Paul normally did his own laundry but knowing that it made his mother feel needed to do it, he always managed to save some for her, even if only towels and washcloths. "There's only one load, Mom, nothing major. I'll bring it. We can put it on to wash then dry after lunch. Do you need anything?"

"Just you."

Her wistful tone tugged at his heart.

"Put on your favorite dress and I'll be right there."

Wishing things were different with his mother did Paul no good. They were as they were. His father's death fifteen years ago had left her slightly unstable. Age, grief, and loneliness added to her infirmity, and resulted in the early stages of dementia.

Despite this, she remained fiercely independent. She absolutely refused to move out of his childhood home and into a retirement residence or nursing facility. Nor would she even contemplate moving in with him, insisting that he needed privacy if he were to ever consider getting himself a wife and blessing her with grandchildren. Her most fervent wish, he knew.

To make things easier for her and less worrisome for himself, Paul paid a home health nurse to go twice a day and make sure she took her medication. Contrary to her claim otherwise, he called her daily and visited at least once a week.

****

Jessica slipped into the church and found an

empty pew. A trip to New Orleans wasn't complete without a visit to the St. Louis Cathedral. Though not a member of the Catholic faith by origin or design, she attended services on occasion and found the celebration of Mass a timeless and beautiful ceremony. Today, she sat in hopeful anticipation of a revelation from God. Today, she expected to get her answer.

For months, God had dealt with her to switch genres in her writing. To change from her normal vein of mysteries and suspense to Christian fiction.

Though she'd always managed to keep the violence in her stories to a minimum, and consciously strove to show that good always triumphs over evil, she'd never thought to weave the faith issue into her plots.

It would be a major change. No doubt one that would cost her since she'd be forced to seek release from her current contract. But she knew the change would be for the betterment of not only her overall life and career, but also her spiritual growth.

She also hoped the change would rid her of Jasper for good.

Jasper Tanner was more than the proverbial thorn in her side. He was a downright nuisance. And, as much as she had once loved him, she now despised him. Not good for spiritual wellbeing, much less growth, she thought as the Mass began.

"Speak of the devil," a voice whispered, as familiar and eerie sensations stole over her. She glanced across the aisle and caught him looking at her. He nodded in greeting. His smile mocked her.

Jessica took a deep breath, forced her gaze forward, closed her eyes and concentrated on the sound of the priest's voice and the prayers he invoked, imploring God's intervention. Though he'd resorted to stalking her, she wasn't afraid of Jasper. Not physically. But the thought of what damage he could do to her career always caused concern.

****

Paul sat with his mother two pews behind Jessica. Though raised in the Church, he only attended Mass on occasion and had no idea what drew him to do so today. Until he saw Jessica and the tall, fair man she'd encountered yesterday. *Why was it the three of them were in the same place at the same time two days in a row?* He pondered the question for a few minutes then it dawned on him that somehow their destinies were entwined.

Knowing his mother would sit without

49

complaint as long as he prayed, Paul slid to his knees, rested his chin on clasped hands, and watched them through lowered lids. As the service neared the end, he noticed how Jessica would glance in the guy's direction then quickly away, bowing her head as though in deep prayer. He watched as the man stood with the crowd and slid out behind the procession, passing Jessica with a brush of his hand on her shoulder.

She recoiled with a visible shudder.

As long as she stayed on her knees, Paul stayed on his. When she rose, so did he. He stepped from the pew and stopped her exit with an outstretched hand. "So, we meet again."

Jessica hesitated but a moment before she grasped his hand in return.

"May I say how thoroughly I enjoyed *Twilight Sorcery*."

Jessica regarded him a minute, wondering if he were sincere or if he offered the same empty flattery other men resorted to. She perceived his honesty and smiled. "Did you figure it out before the end?"

She disengaged her hand from his grasp.

Paul shook his head, grinned. "No. And that surprises me. I don't often get the chance to read for pleasure and have stayed away from mysteries and thrillers because I usually figure out whodunit within a chapter or two. But you had me guessing right up to the end."

An older woman approached them. Paul turned to her and offered his hand. "Mother, I'd like you to meet Miss Jessica Aucoin. She's the author I told you about earlier."

He turned back to Jessica. "Mom's an avid reader too. Though she chooses lighter subjects, prefers short stories and anthologies."

"I lose my train of thought if it's too long," his mother explained as Jessica shook her hand. "Would you like to join us for dinner, dear?"

Caught off guard, Jessica cleared her throat. "Well..." she hesitated, waiting for Paul's reaction to the unexpected invitation.

Paul chortled as if he were not surprised by his mother's question. "I'm sure Miss Aucoin has other plans, but if not, you are welcome to join us."

He'd offered her an out, but also an invitation. Still unsettled by Jasper, she considered accepting, but then thought better of it. Paul was probably simply being polite.

She declined dinner, and turned to leave, still a little unsure of herself—of Jasper, and where he might show up.

She hesitated for a moment and was relieved when Paul stepped up and suggested they give her a ride back to the hotel.

****

Monday morning dawned bright and early. Paul groaned and slapped the alarm off. He'd read too late again. He rubbed his tired eyes and searched his mind to see if there were any major appointments on his calendar, anything he could cancel.

Never one for taking the easy way out, he rolled out of bed, stumbled to the kitchen, and poured a cup of coffee. Thank God he'd thought to prepare the pot and set the timer on automatic. Sitting at the table, he skipped the bible verse and went straight to prayer. He repented his lack of discipline and begged for grace and energy to get through the day.

He'd have to stay away from her books if he was to have a life.

Or get it over with and read them all. He made a mental note to go to the bookstore sometime today to pick up, or order, the rest of her titles.

Though warm and muggy, he welcomed the fresh air and surge of energy that resulted from his normal run. Arriving at the office with minutes to spare, Paul nodded a greeting to his secretary then poured himself a cup of coffee.

"Morning, Debra. Coffee?"

"No thanks," Debra replied, while she gathered his messages.

When he strode into his office, she followed, filling him in on his activities for the day. They had been seated less than five minutes when a noise sounded at the door–a tiny shriek followed by a curse then a groan. Debra turned, displeasure etched in every plane of her face and rose from her chair.

"May we help you?"

Paul stood also. He looked over Debra's shoulder and couldn't help but grin. "Well just fall on in here."

The woman seemed to have a bit of trouble staying on her feet.

Jessica cleared her throat, her cheeks flaming. "I'm sorry if I interrupted. There was no one at the desk."

Debra harrumphed. "Most people would have waited."

Paul gave her a measured look, shocked at the venom in her muttered comment, and then turned his attention back to Jessica. "Do you have an appointment?"

Jessica shook her head. "No, but I was hoping to make one. Unless you can see me now?"

Paul flipped through his messages. "Debra?"

Debra turned back to face him her lips pursed in disapproval. "You're free until ten o'clock."

Paul nodded. "If you'll give us a few more minutes to finish up here, I'll see you then."

"Thanks." Bending, Jessica picked up her shoe and the heel she'd broken and limped back to the lobby.

Paul waited until he was sure Jessica was out of earshot then addressed his secretary. "Want to tell me what's bothering you?"

He saw the quick flash of emotions in Debra's eyes before she dropped her gaze and cringed. Squaring her shoulders, she pasted a cheerful smile on her face and shrugged.

"Typical Monday morning blues, I guess. I'll apologize."

Paul hesitated in reaching out, nodded instead. "Give me five will you?"

Debra inclined her head in agreement and closed the door behind her. When she was gone, Paul indulged himself in a few moments of pure emotion. He'd often suspected Debra's feelings went beyond that of loyal secretary and friend, though she'd never spoken the words aloud. For that he was grateful. He cared about her deeply, respected her more, but she didn't move him the way a wife or possible wife should.

Whatever that means.

A nagging little voice insisted he might miss out on a good thing while holding out for some fairytale emotion to sweep him away. He forced his mind off of that tangent and prayed that the Lord would send Debra someone special. A knock on the door interrupted his thoughts.

"Come in." He rose from his seat. The instant Jessica entered he knew exactly what the words *fairytale emotions* meant. Shaking off the feelings, he waved her into a chair, and then took his own again. "What can I do for you?"

"I'd like you to get me out of my publishing contract."

"Why on earth would you want to do that?"

Her chin jerked up. "Because it's not what I want to write anymore."

Paul leaned back in his chair. "You're going to have to explain that to me before I deign to even consider the possibility."

He left late for his ten o'clock appointment, his mind awhirl. They'd covered a lot of information in an hour-and-a-half. So much so, he wished he could cancel the rest of his day to do the research he needed to help Jessica out of the dilemma she was in, instead of leaving it to Debra.

His reputation as a winner, champion for the underdog, hadn't come without a price, specifically, hours upon hours of research. A task he gladly handed over whenever possible. But this case was a whole new venture for him.

Entertainment Law was something he'd touched on briefly during his years as a lawyer and professor, but not in any depth. Definitely not the depth he needed to take on this case. When he'd mentioned that to Jessica, and offered to refer her to an acquaintance, she'd refused, determined that he be the one to save her.

Nothing like a damsel in distress to bring out the macho in a man.

Forcing his thoughts into some semblance of order, he managed to get through the rest of his meetings and appointments, as well as his evening class. Arriving home a little past nine, he grabbed a bite to eat then booted up his computer. He checked his email for the information he'd asked Debra to send over, printed it out and followed up with more research, making notes as he went.

He finally tumbled into bed well past midnight, his mind still circling from the information he'd discovered. He couldn't wait for the week to pass so he could meet with Jessica again.

****

With care, Jessica dressed for her meeting with Paul in a flowery peasant skirt, simple white blouse, and sandals. No heels today. She hated heels, always had, wondering why women put themselves through such torture. For her, sandals, boots, or maybe an occasional pair of sensible pumps sufficed.

Pulling her thick hair up into a ponytail, she tied a matching scarf around it and studied her reflection. Other than a touch of mascara to separate and lengthen her long, dark lashes, no makeup was necessary. Despite the fact she'd slept only in snatches while holed up in her hotel room all week, her complexion was fairly bright.

The week had actually been exhilarating, as though the minute she quit fighting the Holy Spirit, He'd lent wings to her words. A story had never flowed as freely as this one. Her fingers flew across the keyboard, barely able to keep up with her soaring thoughts. As a result, she nearly had an entire rough draft complete.

All in all, this had been a week well spent, and she hoped Paul would have good news for her this afternoon.

****

Paul studied his notes on Jessica and her case. He'd set her appointment at five o'clock this afternoon for two reasons. One, he'd needed the time to prepare and two he wanted no interruptions. *Like the one now.* "Come in."

Debra entered. "You sure you don't need me to hang around?"

"No. Thank you."

"OK. The coffee pot is ready in case you want some later. All you have to do is turn it on."

Paul noticed her hesitance and put down his notes with a sigh. He needed to talk to her, had put it off all week. "Can we talk a minute?"

Had he been interested her smile would have sealed his fate. His heart thudded with dread when she perched herself on the edge of the chair and clasped her hands in her lap.

Paul inhaled sharply, folded his hands on the desk and prayed for guidance, wisdom, and direction, but most of all, gentleness. "Debra, you know I value you as a secretary."

She nodded.

"And I hope you know how much I enjoy and appreciate your friendship."

She nodded again, blinked fast and swallowed hard.

Paul's heart cringed. "I hope you know I'd never want to disrespect, dishonor or hurt you in any way," he continued, silent prayers going up with each breath as he searched for the words to let her down gently.

Again, Debra nodded, her lips pursed, eyes filled with pain and devastation, yet she uttered not a word.

"You're not going to make this easy for me, are you?" Paul muttered, and then smiled to soften his next words.

"As much as I value you, Debra, we can never be more than friends. I'm sorry if I've ever led you to believe otherwise, but..." He trailed off when a single tear escaped her rigid gaze.

Debra swiped the tear away in an angry gesture. "I know that."

"I don't want to lose you, Deb, but..."

Her chin jerked up. Eyes narrowed. "Are you warning me or firing me?"

Paul shook his head in quick denial. "Neither. You didn't let me finish." He let out a deep breath. "I don't want to lose you. But I'll understand if you want to look for another position."

Debra stood and tossed the hair off her shoulders with an angry shake of her head. "Did I say I wanted to do that?"

Paul rose also, surprised at the vehemence of her reaction. "No."

"Then don't put words in my mouth or ideas in my head. I can accept the fact that I've been a fool, Paul. But I can't accept the fact that you think so little of me, or think *I* think so little of myself, that I can't handle rejection. Even from the likes of you."

Her eyes were nothing more than tiny slits of fire. Paul cleared his throat, drew in a deep, calming breath through clenched teeth, and counted to ten. "I never thought that. My mistake."

Debra nodded. "Good. Then we understand each other?"

"Perfectly."

"Fine. Do you need anything before I go?"

He shook his head. "No but thank you."

"I'll see you Monday, then." Debra turned on her heel and marched out of the office.

Paul sank into his chair and blew out his breath. Well, at least she didn't cry and whine and try to make him feel like a heel. No, not Debra. She simply knocked him off his high horse and politely put him in his place, he realized with a grin.

Thank God.

****

Jessica arrived to find Paul pouring a cup of coffee and chuckling. "Someone's in a good mood." A smile tugged at her lips in response to his. *The man's too sexy for words not to mention my peace of mind.*

"Good afternoon. Coffee?"

"No, thank you."

"C'mon in." He led the way to his office.

"Said the spider to the fly," she mumbled to herself, wondering what had the man so tickled.

Paul waved for her to be seated and took his own once she settled into a chair. "How was your week?"

"Good and yours?"

Another laugh escaped his smiling lips. "Ending with a bang."

Jessica tilted her head and waited for him to elaborate.

"Just had an enlightening conversation with my secretary."

"Where is she?"

"Gone. It's not unusual for me to have late appointments."

Her heart jumped into her throat. "So, we're alone?"

Paul eyed her, a curious lift to his brow. "Does that bother you?"

She smiled, sat back in her chair, and forced herself to relax. "Not unless you bite." *Or weave tangled webs.*

He chortled and loosened his tie. "Not prone to. But who knows when the urge might overtake me."

She couldn't help but giggle.

Paul picked up his notes, sipped his coffee. Silence stretched between them.

"What did you find out?"

"Quite a bit. You want the good news first or the bad?"

"Give me the bad."

He grinned. "Well, it's not really all that bad. I've read your contract and consulted with the legal department of your publisher. There's no way they're going to let you out of it. You're too valuable to them. The only option is for them to reject your next manuscript. However, there may be another solution."

The comment got her full attention.

Paul leaned back in his chair and regarded her over steepled fingers. "Did you know that the marketing director has been urging the publisher to start an inspirational line?"

"You're kidding?"

Excitement colored her cheeks. Hope brightened her eyes. Paul's breath stuck in his throat. He cleared it, took another sip of coffee.

"I kid you not. As a matter of fact, your editor has been pushing for the same thing. My suggestion is that you write the next novel you've contracted keeping that in mind and submit it to them. You wanting to write in this genre will likely be the impetus for them to open the line. There's no guarantee, mind you, but it's worth a shot. The most they can do is to reject the manuscript, the least force a rewrite."

"Oh, wow! I never thought. I mean… That never occurred to me… I should have known, though, the Lord always makes a way. I don't know why I ever doubted."

Her laughter, full, joyous, and carefree feathered over him like a soft caress. The air around her vibrated with enthusiasm. Paul's heart jumped into high gear, his hormones into overdrive. Every muscle in his body tensed with the effort it took to resist the urge to get up and sweep her into his arms.

He took another sip of coffee, hoping the strong, aromatic flavor would curb his need. It was cold, tasted like ashes, and caused his next words to come out with a bitter sting. "Your contract was simple. Jasper Tanner is another matter altogether."

Her breath caught in an audible hiss. The smile fell from her face.

"Why didn't you mention him on Monday?" Paul noted the sudden pallor to her skin. The phone rang before she could respond. He picked it up, wondering who would be calling this late. "Hello?"

"Mr. Seville, its Norma."

Paul sat straighter, instantly alert at hearing the voice of the home health nurse he'd hired to check on his mother. "What is it?"

"It's your mother. I came to check on her as usual and found her extremely disorientated. She's incoherent, lethargic, and slipping in and out of consciousness. I've called an ambulance, the paramedics are loading her up now, and we're on our way to the hospital."

"I'll meet you there." Paul fumbled to hang up the phone, struggled to stand on knees weakened with fright. "I'm sorry. We have to continue this another time. Call my secretary on Monday to reschedule."

"What's wrong?" She stepped in front of him, halting his departure. "Paul, what's wrong?"

He struggled to breathe, forced down the panic clamoring in his throat, fished in his pocket for his keys—which he promptly dropped—then bent to pick them up with a curse. "It's my mother. The home health nurse found her incapacitated. I have to go."

"I'll drive you." Jessica took the keys from his inept fingers.

Paul didn't argue. He simply handed over the keys and rushed to the parking garage with her right on his heels.

They arrived at the hospital minutes after the ambulance. Paul rushed into the emergency room where nurses and doctors were questioning the paramedics and Norma.

"Norma, what's wrong? What happened?"

She stepped away from the gurney, pulling Paul with her outside the cubicle. "I'm not sure, but it appears she's slipping in and out of consciousness due to low blood sugar. That sometimes happens with diabetics."

"*What?!* She doesn't have diabetes."

"Yes, Paul. She does."

The blood drained from his face. The room swam before his eyes. He rubbed them, pinched the bridge of his nose, and struggled to haul in a breath. "Since when?"

Norma eyed him with more than a hint of concern in her eyes. "For about six months now. I'm surprised you didn't know."

He shook his head. "What would cause this to happen?"

"Blood sugar too high, or, as in your mother's case, extremely low."

"And what would cause it to be extremely low?"

"Too much insulin in the bloodstream."

"I'm almost afraid to ask," Paul muttered.

"Me too. She was fine when I checked on her this morning. Her blood sugar was good. I don't think she'd take a shot on her own, but who knows? She seems to be more and more absentminded lately." Norma rubbed at the tension creasing her brow.

"I don't even know if she ate properly after I gave her the shot this morning. She assured me she would, but I couldn't stay to make sure, and without adequate nutrition, the insulin has nothing to process. That too can cause the blood sugar to drop substantially. Lately, I've been thinking that I should take her medications with me when I leave, just to be safe. Now I wish I had. If only I'd stayed and at least made her eat." She buried her face in her hands.

Paul patted her shoulder but refrained from comment. He didn't want to lay blame for something that was clearly not Norma's fault. But, in his present state of mind, he doubted he could say anything that wouldn't add to her guilt, much less relieve it.

Walking back to the cubicle, he stood slightly inside the curtain and watched while the doctors and nurses worked on his mother... Taking vital signs, drawing blood, hooking up IVs.

Oh, God, I'm not ready to let her go, yet. Please don't make me.

When she stirred and mumbled his name, Paul moved closer and took her hand. "I'm here, Mom. I'm here. Hang on."

The minutes dragged by at an agonizing pace. Paul prayed with each tick of the clock. He had no idea whether moments or an eternity passed but was by her side the moment Rosalie opened her eyes, more alert than she'd been since the whole ordeal began.

"Paul? What are you doing here? It's not Sunday, is it?"

His hands shook when he brushed the hair back off her face. "No, Mom. It's not Sunday. It's Friday evening. How are you feeling?"

"Tired." She sighed, closing her eyes. They flew open, instantly aware. "Where am I? What's going on?"

"You're in the emergency room, Mom. Your blood sugar dropped to dangerous levels. Why didn't you tell me you were diabetic?"

Her eyes narrowed. Cheeks flushed. "Because I am not diabetic. I keep telling that woman Jesus has healed me, but she won't believe me. Just keeps giving me those shots. You have to make her stop, Paul. I don't need them anymore."

Paul frowned, but refrained from questioning her further when she closed her eyes once more. "I'll talk to her. You rest now."

He sat by the bed with her hand in his when someone touched his shoulder and whispered his name. Not until that moment did he remember Jessica had been in the waiting room. He turned, rising as he did so, and bumped into her. The shock of contact seared the greeting from his tongue.

Jessica stepped back. "How is she?"

"She's OK. Better. I am so sorry. I forgot about you being here. Let me call a cab for you, or..." His words halted when she placed a finger on his lips.

"It's OK. Don't fret. Are they going to admit her or what?"

Paul shook his head. "I don't know yet."

"Can I get you something, coffee or juice?"

Again, he shook his head. "No. Thank you."

"Well, hello, dear." His mother's voice stopped further conversation. She held out a hand to Jessica. "It's so nice of you to come," she continued, when Jessica took it. "Did you two come together?"

"Yes, Ma'am. How are you feeling?"

"Oh, I'm so glad! I knew you were special the first time I saw you. You two go on now and continue your date. I'll be fine."

Paul chuckled as color infused Jessica's cheeks. "It wasn't a date Mom. We had a business meeting."

"Oh, pooh." She waved a hand at him. "I know the flush of love when I see it, and it's written all over her face."

Paul shook his head. "More like embarrassment. Besides, we hardly know each other."

"That's nonsense. I fell in love with your father the moment I laid eyes on him, and he, me. All this malarkey about finding your soul mate is ridiculous. You know your soul mate the minute you meet them. Now, go." She closed her eyes to signify the end of the conversation.

Paul brushed his lips over her cheek, then took Jessica gently by the arm, and escorted her out of the room. "I'm sorry. She always seems to put you on the spot."

"It's OK. I wish I had a mother to fuss over me like that."

The wistful tone tugged at his heart. Paul knew from his research that Jessica's mother had died when she was thirteen, after which various housekeepers and nannies raised her. Her father, a busy politician, reportedly loved her, but was unable to devote the time necessary to nurture a teenage daughter. He smiled. "Would you like for me to call you a cab?"

Jessica hesitated in answering. The last thing she wanted was to spend the evening with only her characters for company. What she really wanted was to hang around and see how his mother fared. But how could she tell him that? Before she had a chance to worry over the words, a physician approached them.

"Mr. Seville?"

Paul shook the proffered hand. "Yes."

"I'm Dr. Edwards. I'll be keeping an eye on your mother this evening. I'm sure you have a lot of questions, so I'll do my best to answer them. Your mother was on the verge of a diabetic coma, which resulted from low blood sugar. We've got it up now, and she's stable. But I'd like to keep her overnight and run a few tests."

"What kind of tests?"

"Well, the comprehensive blood glucose tests we've run shows her sugar levels have been on the low end of normal for three months. Which is the goal of diabetics. However, in her ramblings both in the ambulance and here, she said she was healed. I'd like to run blood glucose tests periodically throughout the evening and night. After she eats, as well as another comprehensive or two." He waited a beat, and continued when Paul didn't question him.

"If her levels stay low, I'm going to recommend no more insulin injections. I will, however, prescribe a fast acting shot for the instance that it is high and remains high for any length of time. She should be able to go home tomorrow, but her blood sugar levels will have to be checked at least three times a day for a while."

"That's no problem. We already employ a

home health nurse."

Dr. Edwards nodded in approval. "Good. If they go up and stay up, she'll need to see her regular doctor as soon as possible. I'm going to fax these reports over to him on Monday. Other than that, she should be fine."

"Thank you." Paul shook the man's hand again and then turned to Jessica when the doctor entered his mother's room. "The offer of a cab is still open. Unless you'd rather have dinner."

She smiled. "I'd love to. But no talking business."

"You've got a deal."

His grin, charming, boyish, *lethal,* touched her like no other had. Her heart made a slow swirl into her stomach, executed a happy little flip, and settled there.

****

Saturday morning, Paul paced the corridor outside his mother's hospital room instead of enjoying his normal morning run. The night had not been a peaceful one. Nurses were in and out of his mother's room, checking her vital signs and drawing blood.

Now, he was anxious to get home, take a run, get a shower, and then call Jessica. *To report his mother's progress, of course.*

Paul sniggered to himself at the lie, hoping she'd requested the call for the same reasons he wanted to make it. Dinner last night had been sweet, slightly romantic, and not at all awkward.

His heart stuttered as it had each time he thought about her—which was nearly every moment since they met. Everything about the woman touched something deep inside, and he wondered if she was what his heart had been searching for. *His soul mate.*

He closed his eyes, inhaled slow and deep, and felt the truth all the way to his toes. Never one for the fanciful, but rather always practical, he wondered how he'd fallen so deeply so fast. The revelation that he loved her incited more primitive emotions and brought to light unanswered questions.

As agreed, they hadn't talked about business last night, but uncertainty plagued him now. He wanted to know who Jasper Tanner was and what kind of hold he had over Jessica.

Hearing footsteps and his name called, Paul turned and waited as Norma approached.

"How is she?"

"She's fine. The doctor only kept her overnight to run some tests. She should go home sometime today."

"What kind of tests?"

"Well, seems he took her ramblings about being healed seriously. He decided to run periodic glucose tests throughout the evening and night."

"What did they show?"

Before Paul could answer, Dr. Edwards approached them. "Well, she shows no signs of being diabetic. We'll watch her throughout the day, but I'm sure everything will remain the same. She'll be released this afternoon."

Paul thanked him again then turned to Norma, his brow arched in expectation.

"Oh, Paul, I'm so sorry. I've been a nurse for over twenty years and never heard of such a thing."

"She's been a Christian for over forty years."

Norma drew herself to her full five-feet-six-inch height. "Do you want me to recommend another nurse?"

Paul saw the apprehension in her eyes and shook his head. "No, Norma. I don't want another nurse. I want your guarantee you'll take her seriously if she ever starts talking like this again, though."

"You can be assured I will. I mean, I've *heard* of miracle healings, but never dreamed I'd witness one."

"Is checking on her three times a day going to be a problem for you?"

"Not a bit. Do you mind if I visit with her now?"

"Not at all. I need to get home anyway. Mom, look who's here to see you." Stepping back, Paul allowed Norma to enter first.

"Hi, Rosalie, I hear you've received a miracle!"

His mother beamed in response. Paul took her hand in his then kissed her cheek. "I need to go home for a while, Mom. I'll see you later."

She smiled. "Get some rest. And bring that pretty writer back with you this afternoon. I'd like to get to know her better."

Paul laughed at the command. "Me too, Mom. Me too."

Three hours later he slammed down the phone with disgust. He'd been unable to reach Jessica all morning. Frustrated at the lack of progress in getting answers to his questions about Jasper Tanner, he'd searched the Internet, but found nothing substantial.

Deciding it could wait until he saw her again, he left his apartment with the intent to return to the hospital to await his mother's release. He arrived to find her and Jessica twittering over a story his mother had read in the latest anthology she'd purchased.

"Oh, Paul, look who's come to visit," Rosalie exclaimed, reaching for his hand, and lifting her cheek for his kiss.

Paul obliged then nodded at Jessica. "No wonder I couldn't reach you. I figured you'd be pounding away on the keyboard."

"Couldn't concentrate."

"Makes two of us." Lame, he thought. *Sound and feel like a teenager in the throes of his first crush.*

Rosalie's voice interrupted his musings. "Why don't you two go have lunch somewhere? I'm kind of tired."

Paul snickered. "You shouldn't be so subtle, Mother."

She flushed. "And you shouldn't be so uppity, young man. I'm not too old or too feeble to take you to task. I'm simply trying to be mindful of the fact that I interrupted your business meeting yesterday and offering you the chance to continue it."

Paul doubled over with mirth. "Right," he breathed, wiping tears of hilarity off his cheeks. "And I'm the Pope."

"You see what I have to put up with?" She turned an imploring gaze at Jessica. "An ungrateful and disrespectful son."

"You should be ashamed of yourself," Jessica chided.

Though she tried to tease, Paul heard the sharp stab of longing in her voice. He held a hand out to her. "Scold me over lunch."

Jessica hesitated but a moment before taking it. "Where are we going?" she asked moments later when he pushed the button for the elevator.

"Out. The cafeteria's atmosphere is about as good for conducting business as its fare."

Before she could respond, the elevator doors swooshed open. Thrilled to find they were alone; it took every ounce of self-control Paul possessed not to push the emergency stop button and corner her in the tiny booth. When the doors opened to let them out into the covered parking garage, he wondered why he'd hesitated. Keeping her hand firmly in his, he led her over to his car.

Fishing in his pocket for his keys, he pressed the remote button and unlocked the car. When he stepped back to open the door, his body brushed hers just lightly enough to send lightening sparks of desire shooting through his entire system, galvanizing him in their wake.

"One kiss," he murmured, and cupped her face in his hand while lowering his lips to hers in a thorough caress. By the time he regained his senses, Jessica lay plastered against him, her hands fisted in his hair, his arm like a steel manacle around her waist.

Parting was actually painful.

Released from his strong embrace, Jessica leaned against the sleek BMW for support. He stepped back, her cheek still cupped in one hand, her waist in the other. A myriad of emotions glittered in his dark gaze. Her finger on his lips stopped the apology hovering there. She shook her head.

"Don't. That's the kind of kiss I've searched for my entire life," she admitted, her voice low and filled with awe. Something in her words must have struck a chord. Paul stiffened, took another step back, dropping his hand from her waist then face.

"Really?"

She nodded.

"Then who the hell is Jasper Tanner and what does he want?"

Jessica fought the tremble of trepidation, which threatened to weaken her already shaky legs. The time had come for truth. She laid her hand against his cheek, thrilled when he didn't pull away. "Take me someplace quiet, where we can talk, and I'll tell you a story."

Paul guided her onto the passenger seat, closed the car door then walked around to the driver's side and climbed in beside her. The engine purred to life with a single stroke of the ignition.

A heavy silence accompanied them on the

drive, followed them into the restaurant and hung over their table like a nasty cloud. Thick. Odorless. Deadly.

Jessica waited until Paul had ordered the wine before deigning to speak. She studied him for a moment, the strands of silver slipping like wisps of smoke through his dark hair, the brooding midnight eyes, and the sensual mouth. She could all but feel his impatience, tightly leashed, and smiled.

"Once upon a time there was a lonely princess..." She let her words trail off when his eyebrow shot up in surprise.

"A princess?"

"It's my story, I'll tell it as I please."

Paul nodded, took a sip of his wine, and sat back in his chair. Jessica knew there were no pretty words to dress up this story. *Best to just get it out in the open.* She opened her mouth, but Paul's cell phone chimed.

He reached for it. "I'm sorry. I have to take this. I'm waiting for a call from a judge."

It wasn't the judge. Though static muffled the caller's voice, Paul understood the word 'wife.' He moved the phone to his other ear and tried to listen to the caller's mumbling.

"I'm sorry, you're breaking up. What did you say?"

"I said, stay away from my wife."

"Who is this?"

"You know who this is. Consider yourself warned."

The phone went silent. Paul shook his head and frowned. He checked the caller ID, but the information had been blocked. He turned his attention back to Jessica, "Must have been a wrong number. Some nut telling me to stay away from his wife. I'm sorry, go back to what you were telling me."

"Jasper Tanner is my husband."

The admission got his full attention. Paul nearly choked on his wine.

"What did you say?"

"Call it childhood folly, teenage madness, a huge mistake and a total disaster."

"After that kiss we shared and what you said, I'd call it adultery."

Emotions flickered over her face. Her hand trembled when she took a sip of wine. "Will you sit in judgment, Paul, over a slip of sanity on the part of a fifteen-year-old girl, or would you rather hear the whole story first?"

He had hurt her. He could see that, and it bothered him, but he couldn't help it. She'd lied, and the betrayal tore him up inside.

****

Noxious silence followed them back to the hospital. Jessica wanted to know his thoughts but was too afraid to ask. Ridicule and judgment she'd endured in spades since that fateful day when a lonely girl–child really–ran off with the one she thought to be her knight in shining armor. The woman in her mourned the destruction of that fantasy, while the girl in her still searched for her hero, the one man who would love her and fulfill those youthful dreams of happy-ever-after.

He would have to be a strong man, her hero. One who could stand up to Jasper and put an end to his mischief and vengeful attempts to humiliate, disgrace, and discredit her, since the dissolution of their marriage.

She remembered the pleasure, the total abandonment she felt in Paul's arms less than two hours ago and wondered if he were the champion of her dreams. He was certainly strong enough, intelligent enough, and handsome enough.

Hope flared in her spirit, curled around her dreams, and slipped through the doubts in her mind. Her heart did a little happy dance then settled like a dead weight in her stomach.

Paul was everything she'd ever wanted in a man, but would he take on the challenge her shattered dreams presented?

They arrived in the parking garage. He escorted her to her car, and promised to give her a call soon, but she wasn't sure he would.

****

Paul's mind whirled at what all Jessica had revealed to him. Although he'd never spoken to the man, there was no doubt in his mind that the phone call he received came from Jasper Tanner. The memory of her reaction to Tanner at the bookstore, and church, led credence to her claims of harassment and stalking.

Determination replaced the anger and betrayal he initially felt. He vowed to get to the bottom of the situation and see what he could do to free her from Jasper's clutches for good. He returned to his mother's room to find her ready and waiting to be released.

"Where's Jessica?"

"Gone back to her hotel."

"Something's wrong. What is it, Paul?"

Despite her sketchy memory, her powers of observation hadn't dimmed. Nor had her intuition. Paul closed his eyes and hissed in a breath. "Nothing for you to worry about. Where do you want to go, home or my place?"

"Home. Then I want you to go meet Jessica, and get whatever it is that happened at lunch, straightened out."

"Wish it were that simple, Mom. But it's not. Besides, the doctor said your blood sugar needs to be checked regularly, so I'm staying with you the rest of the weekend. Norma will take over again on Monday."

She scoffed. "That's nonsense and unnecessary. When the Lord heals, He heals completely."

"Maybe so, Mom. But if that's true, why hasn't He healed you of your other ailments?"

"What ailments?"

"The doctor says you have the early stages of dementia."

She waved his words away. "Oh, pooh. More nonsense. There's nothing wrong with me that a good old-fashioned dose of life can't help. There's no cure for loneliness, Son, except family. Which is exactly why you need to settle down and give me some grandchildren to spoil."

Paul smiled down at her. "I'm working on it, Mom. Always open to the idea. The right woman hasn't come along, yet." *Until now*. He kept that thought to himself.

When the orderly appeared to wheel his mother out, Paul went to bring the car around to the hospital entrance. He waited until they were on their way to her house before continuing the conversation.

"If you're so lonely, Mom, why won't you consider moving into a retirement community or home?"

"I do not want to live with a bunch of strangers."

"Aren't you the one who always said that a stranger is merely a friend in disguise?"

She rolled her eyes. "I hate it when you do that."

"What?" He tried to sound innocent.

"Use my own words against me."

He chuckled. "It's the law, Mom. Anything you say can and will be used against you."

She snorted.

"Seriously though, moving might be the best thing. There are communities where you can have your own home or an apartment where you can be closer to others. There's an activity center with get-togethers planned for everyone, and always someone nearby."

"And what would I do with all this?" She waved her hand to encompass her home and property as Paul pulled into the driveway.

Paul waited until he'd settled her on the couch, and himself in the recliner, to continue the conversation. "We've been over this before, Mom. You can sell the house and property. Or I'll buy you a home wherever you want and keep this. Your choice."

"My choice is to stay here, where I've lived most of my life. There's plenty of room for you to build your own home on this land, and we'll all be together as a family should. Case closed." She held up a hand to signify the conversation's end.

Paul shook his head and refrained from commenting. This was one argument he'd never win, and he knew better than to say another word.

****

Monday morning dawned bright and early. Dressed in a pair of jogging shorts and a T-shirt, Paul took his daily run around his old neighborhood. Not much had changed since he lived here as a boy. On one level, he understood why his mother didn't want to leave. On the other hand, one couldn't stop life, and sometimes life required change. That thought rolled into another and quickly progressed to the situation with Jessica.

Paul finished his run, showered, and dressed for work. He had breakfast with his mother. When Norma arrived, he went over the glucose journal they'd kept with her. Promising to call and check on her later, he left his mother's, and went straight to the office, relieved to find he had a relatively light caseload for the day.

Instructing that he was not to be disturbed unless his mother, her nurse, or Jessica called, Paul closed the door behind him and went to work, anxious to see what he could discover.

Two-and-a-half hours later, he was in a much better frame of mind. Things weren't as hopeless as he thought. Before he could pick up the phone to call Jessica, there was a knock on his door.

"You've a visitor. I told her you'd be leaving soon, in ten minutes to be exact," Debra said, consulting her watch. "But she insists on seeing you."

"Who is it?"

"Jessica Aucoin."

"Send her in." The door hadn't had time to close on Debra's departing figure when Jessica walked through it. Paul stood and walked around his desk to meet her. ""Hey. I was about to call you."

Jessica stiffened, and stepped back, as he reached for her. "I came to say good-bye."

"But I have good news for you."

She shook her head. "You've made it painfully obvious that you're not happy with the situation—a situation that I can't change by the way. So, I'm going home. Thank you for the help with my contract. I'll pay your secretary on my way out."

Before she could escape through the door, Paul stepped around her and slammed it shut. His eyes narrowed into tiny slits. "Just like that? You dump all this on me then run off like some coward before we can even discuss it? I don't think so. Not after Saturday. Not after what we shared."

Debra's voice cut off Jessica's response. "You've a call on line one. Person says it's urgent."

Paul swore and stepped over to the desk to take the call. "Don't move."

Jessica listened to his end of the conversation with mounting dread, his answers giving credence to its subject. When he turned to her, his face a mask of frustration and fury, she had no doubt the call was either about, or *was*, Jasper.

"Will you hold the line a minute," she heard Paul bark as she slipped through the door.

"Jessica, wait!"

She turned on him in an angry whirl. "Why? So, you, too, can tell me how foolish and irresponsible I've been? Don't you think I know that by now? But I can't change the past, and I can't seem to do anything about the present!"

He opened his mouth, and then closed it

again, before turning to his secretary who was staring at them with a mixture of concern and curiosity.

"Get on line one and take a number then reschedule everything else for today. I'm going to lunch with the Board of Directors of Loyola then taking the afternoon off."

"What do you want me to tell them?"

He fairly growled. "I don't care what you tell them. Reschedule."

He took Jessica by the arm, his movements, decisive. His grip gentle, he escorted her to the parking garage. He turned her to face him, his hands resting lightly on her waist. "Will you wait and talk to me this afternoon?"

"I've already checked out of the hotel."

"So? Sight see. Go shopping. Visit my mother. Do anything. Just don't leave. If I could get out of this meeting, I would, but I can't. Wait for me. Meet me at Café Du Monde at one o'clock."

Jessica hesitated a moment then nodded.

"Good. Where's your car?"

"Right next to yours."

Only when he'd seen her safely in her car, did Paul allow himself the kiss he so desperately wanted. His lips covered hers in a tender caress and then brushed over her cheek, lingering near her ear. "I'll see you in a while."

He climbed into his car and drove to the meeting, his mind preoccupied with Jessica and Jasper Tanner.

Arriving at the restaurant after everyone else was seated, he apologized for being late, and tried to focus on the discussion around the table. As the meeting wore on, he found himself more and more distracted and unable to concentrate. He excused himself and hurried to Café du Monde, only to find Jessica gone, and a note in her stead.

Paul,

I know that the sins of our past are washed away by the Blood of Jesus to be remembered by God no more. Wish it were that easy for the rest of us. I guess though, that some reap what they sow forever.

PS: I'm afraid I am a coward after all.

Paul felt as though he'd been kicked in the gut. His first instinct was to crumple the note and toss it in the nearest trashcan. The words from the song, *Tear Stained Letter*, traipsed through his mind. Unfolding the page, he smoothed it out as much as possible, noted the splotched ink, read between the lines, and knew that she'd neither been cold nor unemotional at the time of the writing.

And he was not going to let her go that easily.

It took less than two days to rearrange his work and class schedule and make plans for Norma to stay with his mother. Thursday morning, Paul called the office before embarking on his journey to Everglades, Florida. Debra's harried tone sent a shiver of apprehension down his spine.

"I think you'd better come in. There's someone here to see you. He's very insistent."

"Who is it?"

"Jasper Tanner."

"Have him wait in my office, and I'll be right there." Paul turned his car around and made a call to the Chief of Police. A patrol car pulled up to the building within moments of his arrival. Paul consulted with the officers for a minute then went inside.

He stopped at Debra's desk and scribbled *"the police are here"* on a piece of paper, and then entered his domain.

Before Jasper could utter the first whine, Paul pinned him against the wall in a death grip, his teeth clenched as tightly as the fist on Jasper's shirt.

"I'm warning you one time and one time only, quit harassing me and stay away from Jessica."

The police entered as arranged and took Jasper into custody.

****

Spanish moss hung like gossamer curtains in huge Cypress trees. A Roseate Spoonbill rose gracefully from where it had been drinking in her pond. Birds sang their joyous praise. But all Jessica heard was the Mocking bird scolding her.

What have I done?

The fifteen-hour trip from New Orleans had been long and miserable. She'd cried as many tears as the miles she drove. Arriving home in the early hours of Tuesday morning, she'd collapsed into a blue funk unlike any she'd ever known. Depression and misery were her only companions. And more tears than a body should be able to produce.

Curling up in the antique rocker on her porch, Jessica sipped a cup of hot Chamomile tea and watched brilliant orange give way to yellow, gold and peach while the sun slipped from the sky. The moon rose in its place, full and glowing. Stars twinkled to life in the heavens.

Still, she found no peace.

Tears slipped slowly down her cheeks, and she contemplated the mess that was her life. Hearing an approaching vehicle, she put down her now-cold tea, and stood when it turned into her drive. Reaching inside the door, she turned on the porch light as the car came to a halt and the driver disembarked. *What are you doing here?* She wanted to ask but couldn't get the words past the lump of emotion clogging her throat.

Paul watched a kaleidoscope of emotions flitter across her lovely features as he walked up onto the porch–a glimmer of hope, a glint of doubt, a shadow of pain. Stopping an arm's length away, he cupped her cheek in his hand.

"We never did finish our discussion," he murmured and pulled her against his chest as she burst into tears.

"Why are you here?"

"Do you honestly think I'd let the one woman in the world who can move me with a single smile walk away without a by-your-leave?"

"What about Jasper?"

"The marriage wasn't legal, honey. First, you were both minors and second, it wasn't consummated." He eyed her. "Was it?"

She shook her head.

"So, you see, it's not binding, not in the legal sense nor in the biblical. You're a brilliant woman, sweetheart, surely you know that."

"That's what my father says. But Jasper keeps insisting otherwise. He swears the laws of

Nevada, not Florida, are what counts."

"Honey, the man's a nut case. Don't worry, though, I know exactly how to put a stop to the shenanigans of Jasper Tanner."

"How?"

"For starters there's a restraining order..." He let his words trail off when she shook her head.

"I've tried that. He doesn't bother me here, only where it's not enforceable. Then, there are the chat rooms, and message boards, online, where he constantly maligns my reputation."

"Well, then, how about a law suit? Slander, defamation of character, stalking."

"Who would take that case? His father's the Governor of Florida."

"I'd take that case. And I'd win, too. But if you think it's useless, there's only one other solution."

"What?" Hope collided with the doubt in her voice.

"You should get married."

Jessica's lips slowly curled into a smile and then laughter burst forth. "You call that a proposal?"

He grinned, pulled a tiny diamond ring out of his pocket, and dropped to one knee. "No, but this is. Jessica Aucoin, will you marry me?"

Her exuberant response nearly tumbled

them to the floor.

****

Three months later, Jessica tightened Paul's arms around her waist as they watched workmen lay the foundation for their new home. "I still can't believe it."

He rested his cheek against her head. "Believe what?"

"That all it took to get Jasper off my case was to get married. All of the blogs and forums where he posted things against me have been shut down or his posts erased, and I haven't heard from him in months."

Paul chuckled. "I have a confession to make. Jasper showed up at my office the day I left to follow you to Florida."

She turned, her eyes wide. "What happened?"

"I had him arrested. The Judge ordered him to cease and desist all activities against you and to remove all liable and slanderous material he'd posted on the Internet. Otherwise, Jasper would see the inside of a New Orleans jail cell for an undetermined length of time."

She cackled and threw her arms around his neck. "How on earth did you manage all that without me even knowing?"

He twirled her around with a snicker then set her on her feet. "It pays to have connections."

She placed her hand against his cheek and emitted a lusty sigh. Her arms slid around his neck. Her lips reached to receive his kiss. "My hero."

The End

Dear Reader,

We all make mistakes in our lives. Some are easily forgiven though not always quite so easily forgotten. The good news is that the Blood of Jesus washes us as white as snow and God remembers not the sins of our past.

We shouldn't either.

If you don't know Him already, I pray that you will seek to know the Lord Jesus Christ and if you do, that you will pursue a closer walk with Him.

As always may God *BLESS* and keep you and yours always in the palm of His mighty hand!

Paper Roses

Never should have opened the door.

Patti stood, dumbfounded, at the sight before her. Flung about in happy disarray, toilet paper draped every bush and tree on her front lawn.

"Brent!"

Her teenage son bounded down the stairs then froze–mouth open, eyes wide. "They didn't!"

Patti's frown turned into a giggle. "Oh, yes they did."

Remembering her own high school days, she saw the humor in the situation. Rolling yards was a Homecoming tradition. Though she doubted Brent would appreciate the sentiment as he cleaned up the mess. "I'll make breakfast while you call your buddies."

He turned back to the stairs grumbling all the way to his room. Patti wondered how many of the football players would turn out to help with cleanup and whether or not their coach would accompany them. Before she could gather the items she needed for breakfast, her phone rang.

"Morning, Patti," Coach Jude Theriot's voice rang over the line and set butterflies aflutter in her core. "Heard you had some visitors last night."

She laughed. "Quite a few, if my yard is any indication."

His responding chuckle caused her heart to stutter. "We'll be there within the hour to clean up."

"How many should I make breakfast for?"

"Breakfast won't be necessary. Hot chocolate would be appreciated though."

"Done." Patti hung up the phone and Cha-Cha'd across the kitchen floor. Since the day she took Brent to football practice two years ago, Jude Theriot had occupied her mind during the day and graced her dreams at night.

Humming, she set about making breakfast then pulled out ingredients for muffins, hot chocolate, and café au lait–her favorite beverage. She and Brent had finished eating, and the first batch of blueberry and banana nut muffins were in the oven when the doorbell rang.

He's here!

Excitement seized her. Dishes clanged in the sink.

"I got it." Brent pushed away from the table and traipsed through the foyer. His boots clattered against the tile in cadence with the beat of her heart.

Patti heard the door open, voices, and then

cringed when the door slammed. *If that boy doesn't learn how to close a door properly.*

She glanced out the window as the coach and what looked like the entire third string of the football team began picking up paper and cardboard tubes. A thought occurred. She hurried to open the window and yelled, "Save me the rollers that aren't ruined."

She could use them for craft projects with her 1st grade class.

Receiving thumbs up from Jude, she closed the window and continued preparing snacks. She transferred pastries from the oven to a cooling rack then put another batch in to bake.

The boys continued to collect toilet paper off the ground and out of the trees, but every time she glanced out to check their progress, Jude seemed to be preoccupied behind his truck. She watched him walk around, gather a few twigs then return to the open tailgate.

Wonder what he's doing?

Widowed eleven years ago, she doubted she'd ever get over her grief and innate shyness enough to date or fall in love again. Not that she'd had time, really. Finishing her Master's degree while teaching and raising an active boy didn't lend much opportunity for romance.

Until she met Jude.

Her mind continued to circle around the

man who'd snagged her heart and the many conversations they'd shared. For two basically shy people, they never seemed to run out of things to talk about. The occasional brush of hands and long, lingering looks that sometimes passed between them made her wonder if his feelings for her went deeper than that of friend and colleague also. But she could never be so bold as to ask.

She pulled the last batch of muffins out of the oven, turned the burner off under the hot chocolate, and then stirred milk and sugar into a pot of chicory coffee.

She glanced out the window once more to find a clean yard and the boys gathered around their coach as he talked. He gestured then threw back his head and laughed. Her lips twitched in response.

Placing the food and drink on her table in the adjoining dining room, Patti went to the front door to call them in. "Refreshments are ready!"

Whoops and hollers of gratitude were followed by the thunder of feet as the boys scrambled up off the ground and approached the house. "Wash up first. Downstairs bathroom. Food's in the dining room."

Brent led the party to do as she'd bid. Patti waited until the last boy paraded through the door then turned to see where Jude was.

He closed the tailgate, bent to pick something up, then emerged from behind the truck carrying a box.

She smiled. "Find some rollers not ruined?"

He held the box toward her, a twinkle in his eyes. "See for yourself."

Patti opened the container to find a slew of cardboard tubes and a dozen paper roses.

The End

Dear Reader,

How often do we put our lives on hold for others–children, parents, boss, or employees– out of love or obligation or sheer terror of losing? In Patti's case, she let shyness and grief stop her from taking a chance on love. Man was not meant to live life alone and life's much sweeter when you have someone to share it with.

Something to think about...

In His Sight

Lorelei Connor scoured the atlas on the coffee table. Her eyes searched far from the small town where she resided. The tick of the clock on the mantle above the fireplace reminded her time was running out.

Fear crawled up her spine.

They had lived in one place for too long. It was time to move on.

She closed her eyes, placed the red marker over the state of Tennessee and let the Lord lead her hand. She gazed down at the circle southeast of Nashville. *Stars Crossing*. The name leapt out. She did a quick search on the internet for specifics and clicked on the 'Real Estate' link to verify housing was available.

A note on the page caught her eye. *Handyman needed for maintenance and minor repairs of properties owned by agency. Emailed resumes accepted.* Her soul danced in excitement.

She picked up the laptop and rushed into her daughter's room. "Laurel, I know where we're going!"

Her child groaned and buried her face in a pillow. "Not again, Mom. Where to now?"

Lorelei climbed up on the bed and elbowed her in a gentle gesture. "Look at this little town in Tennessee I've discovered."

Laurel sat up and glanced at the screen. "*Stars Crossing?* Whoever heard of Stars Crossing, Tennessee? Stupid name if you ask me. You promised we'd stay here for a while."

Despondency colored her tone and made Lorelei's heart ache. "This time for good. No more moving. You'll see."

"Yeah, like I haven't heard *that* before."

Lorelei closed the laptop and crawled off the bed with a sigh. Weariness dragged at her. She understood how Laurel felt. She too despaired of the constant moving. Maybe this time she'd find the peace she craved and a quiet, unhurried lifestyle where she felt safe.

"Pack up your things."

She returned to the living room and emailed her resume to the real estate agency. Two days later they hit the road, everything they owned in the backseat and trunk of her car. Five days after leaving Wyoming, they arrived in Stars Crossing, Tennessee. Within hours she had a place to live, a job, and Laurel was registered for school.

****

Carson Alexander walked through his classroom and tugged desks into a semi-circle around the dry eraser board. One thing he loved about teaching sixth-grade English at Stars Crossing Middle School was that the classes were so small. With no more than fifteen students at a time he could work closely with each one and give them the attention they needed and deserved.

Another thing he appreciated was the lack of standardized or strict curriculum. As long as the children passed the exams set forth by the Department of Education, he could teach as he pleased.

So far, his kids excelled, maintaining some of the highest scores in the entire school. Pride filled his soul and caused his heart to swell, chest to puff out.

Pride cometh before the fall.

The Voice echoed in his mind, ricocheted through his soul. He shrugged off the warning, walked to his desk and picked up the name tags for his incoming students. He thumbed through the stack, pondered each one and wondered about the child attached to the name... Jenny & Jerry Smith—twins or un-related?

One name struck him hard, sent unknown emotion curling through his system. *Laurel Connor.*

He hadn't heard the name Laurel in years and then used only as a surname or when referring to the small town in Mississippi from whence he came. He moved to Stars Crossing, Tennessee five years ago for two reasons. One, the teaching position and two, the town though smaller, reminded him of home.

Memories crashed through the floodgates he'd built around his heart... The huge, two-story house and two-hundred-acre farm where he grew up. His seven siblings. Parents who adored him. The pain of losing everything he held near and dear to his heart.

Tears threatened. His vision blurred. Hands began to shake. Carson swallowed the lump in his throat, put the stack down, and shoved his hands into the front pockets of his slacks. Adrenaline pumped through him, causing his pulse to skitter and jump. Saliva pooled in his mouth. By sheer force, he willed his emotions under control.

The bell rang and he turned to greet the children who rushed into the room. He watched as one-by-one they filed in and took a seat.

Someone's missing.

He rifled through the name tags then wandered over to the door and saw her, trudging toward the class. Desolation lined every feature of an otherwise lovely face. He turned back to the class and began roll call. He handed each child their student ID and waited for her to enter. The tardy bell rang seconds before she reached for the knob and pulled the door open. All eyes turned. She averted her gaze, mumbled an apology, and slid into the only available seat.

"Hello, Miss Connor." Warmth in his tone eased the frown from her face.

"How'd you know my name?"

He smiled and handed her a name tag. "Only one I had left."

"Oh." She ducked her head at the snickers coming from the other students. A flush darkened her cheeks.

"Enough!"

Everyone jumped to attention. Muffled laughter died.

"One thing I will not tolerate is rudeness especially when it causes disruption in my class or embarrassment to one of my students." One at a time, he met each youngster's gaze until assured his meaning was clear then continued. "We're all equal here, classmates, and we will respect each other."

Relief flickered in her eyes. He smiled down at her, pleased when the corners of her mouth tugged upward in response. Carson walked over to his desk then turned back to address the class.

"I never understood why we start the school year on a Wednesday, but since I can't change that, we're going to spend the next three days getting to know one another. I don't mean by name only. Some of you have lived here your entire lives. Some are new and some have only been in the area a couple of years." He hesitated, picked up a pen and tapped it against his palm.

"What I'd like for each of you to do is write a one-page essay on your life... Who you are, where you're from, what you want to be when you grow up. Keep it brief, concise, and to the point. We'll read them aloud over the next two days. Friday is an open house and I'm looking forward to meeting your parents or guardians. Any questions, don't hesitate to ask."

His eyes met Laurel's. Only a brief moment of contact, but long enough for him to see the sheer panic there. Color rushed to her cheeks. She ducked her head, placed a trembling hand to paper, and began to write.

That afternoon, Carson sat at his desk, head in hands. Along with English, he taught Art and Physical Education. Between the academic subjects and herding a bunch of sixth graders through PE, the first day of school left him exhausted. Added to that, the memories which bombarded him from the moment he picked up Laurel Conner's name tag had haunted him throughout the day.

Anger pummeled through his veins. Slapping his palms down on the desk, he pushed the chair back with such force it toppled, the crash intercepted by the window frame behind his desk. A low growl sounded in his throat. He pivoted on his heel to stare out the glass panes. His stomach roiled. Bile rose in his throat. He swallowed hard and scrubbed the heels of his hands over his face. He ground his teeth until his jaw ached then clenched them in determination.

He would not voice the tragedy aloud. Would not give this thing any more power over him.

Sleep that night was far from peaceful. He awoke more than once drenched in sweat, his heart at a gallop, so fast he thought the organ would explode. He rubbed the spot in his chest until the desperate pace eased then drifted back to hell. When the alarm rang at five a.m., he slapped it off and tumbled from the bed.

On automatic pilot, Carson dressed, downed a glass of juice, and headed out for his morning ride. The sleek mountain bike, fresh air and soft dew refreshed his weary soul and helped him prepare for the day ahead.

****

The children read their essays aloud on Thursday and Friday. Carson picked them up to examine. This would enable him to see which student needed help and where. Whether in basic points of English or specific aspects, he learned a lot about his student's level of understanding from this first assignment of the year.

Laurel's paper reverberated through his brain. He frowned. No doubt she made up most of her life story but why? What could be in the eleven-year-old's past that would make her lie? He'd have to ask her mother at Open House if he wanted to find out the truth. Friday night he waited, even stayed late, but neither Laurel nor her mother showed up at the event.

Saturday morning dawned bright and clear. Brilliant hues of orange and gold splattered across a baby blue sky. Warmth and light bathed the earth in vibrant colors of early fall. Scents perfumed the air as Carson set out on his bike— Pine, Magnolia, Honeysuckle. He breathed deep and picked up his pace.

Over the hump and through the woods to grandmother's house we go. The ditty flitted through his mind and made him chuckle.

Laughter was a welcome relief after the last few days. The start of a new school year was always hectic, and he relished the opportunity to ride away the tension.

He wasn't on his way to grandmother's

house, but to 123 Horseshoe Lane–the address on Laurel Connor's school records. Her mother's name wove through his thoughts and shuddered through his entire being—*Lorelei Connor*. Goosebumps rose on his flesh. He clamped down on the dark emotions swirling and shoved them from his mind.

Rounding a curve, he slowed his bike, and turned into the drive, then stopped to study the tiny home.

His spirits lifted at the sight of the A-frame structure resembling an overgrown dollhouse. Lace-shaped shutters framed pale yellow windows set in vinyl siding a shade creamier. Cheery curtains swayed in the breeze.

A wrap-around porch extended handrails on each side of the steps and welcomed visitors like open arms. Small flowerbeds on either side offered a smorgasbord of fragrance to tease the nostrils.

He pedaled closer, careful not to disturb anything, and dismounted the bike. He snapped the kickstand in place then sauntered to the door and rang the bell. The door opened with a jerk.

"May I help you?"

"Ms. Connor?"

A wary expression crossed her face. "Who's asking?"

He extended a hand toward her. "I'm Carson Alexander. Laurel's English teacher. I'd like to speak with you a moment if it's not too much trouble."

She ignored his outstretched hand, stepped through the entry, and yanked the door shut behind her. "About?"

Surprised at her coldness, he took a step back and allowed his hand to drop to his side. "I asked the students to do an essay on their life so they would know a little more about each other and for me to get an idea of their strengths and weaknesses in English. Laurel's paper was... shall I say... inventive?"

Her eyebrow arched. Annoyance darkened her gaze. "Was there something wrong with the paper, Mr. Alexander?"

"No, the writing is very articulate."

"Then I don't see what the problem is."

He cleared his throat. "The problem is that the entire story is made up. I've taught long enough to know kids will embellish what they consider a boring existence to a certain degree, but I've never had one write an outright fairytale."

"Were there misspelled words, poor sentence structure, or improper grammar?"

He shook his head.

"Then I suggest you concentrate on how

well-versed she is in the English language and not the validity of her life story, which is none of your business, anyway." She turned back into the house and slammed the door in his face.

Carson stood for a full minute before indignation set in. He ground his teeth and fought the urge to knock again. Swiveling on his heel, he tugged the bike from its rest, wrenched the kickstand into place and strode back up the walk. About half-way home the absurdity of what happened struck him. He laughed and slowed his pace.

Boy what a beauty! Raven hair. Crystal-green eyes like her daughter's. Finely chiseled features. Ivory skin. *And a mixture of fire and ice in her veins*. His heart executed a happy little flip. He'd found his woman. All of his life he'd known what kind of woman he wanted as a wife—strong, passionate, and beautiful. Lorelei Connor fit the bill perfectly.

The next morning, he drove to church, surprised, and pleased to see Laurel and her mother seated a few rows ahead of where he sat. No mistaking the identical-shaped heads, similar curve of cheeks, sweep of lashes, mysterious smile. Had he not known better, he'd swear the two were sisters, instead of mother and daughter. The only obvious difference in them besides age was hair color.

Where Laurel sported thick, golden locks tied in a ponytail, her mother's sleek, sable strands were pulled into a French twist. A few errant curls escaped to frame her face and caress the elegant arc of her neck.

His heart hammered against his ribcage; stomach quivered. Apprehension rose to choke him. Carson clutched his hands, sat back, closed his eyes, and fought the demon within.

****

Lorelei stood in the driveway and surveyed the property before her. The tiny log cabin charmed her with its authenticity, but the lawn insulted her landscaper's sensibilities. No flowers or shrubs. No bordered walkway to the house. Not a single item accentuated the beauty of the land on which the cabin stood. She shuddered. Nothing hurt her soul more than to see an undeveloped lawn, especially one with such potential.

"Think you can fix this one up as pretty as you did yours?"

She turned to face the real estate agent who happened to be her landlord as well as her employer. "Depends on who lives here. We'd want the décor to compliment the tenant as well as accentuate the design of the home."

He chuckled. "Since the tenant is a bachelor, I guess you ought not choose those frilly looking shutters."

She smiled. "I have a few ideas. When can I start?"

"Bring your sketches to the office tomorrow morning, early, and we'll decide from there."

The next morning, she arrived at the real estate office within minutes of dropping Laurel off at school. Mr. Flaven led her into a conference room where she spread the sketches out on a large table. She waited while he put a pot of coffee on to brew. He sat across from her and surveyed the various designs. He sat back and contemplated her over steepled fingers, an expression of awe on his face.

"Can you really do all this?"

She nodded. "Depending on which arrangement or combination you approve."

"You sure your title is Landscape Architect and not magician?"

A flush warmed her cheeks. "Not magic, just passion. When other little girls played dolls, I built their houses out of sticks and stones."

He laughed. "I'm sure there's a wealth of passion inside you."

A chill washed over her. She shifted in her chair and crossed her arms over her chest. Something in her demeanor must have alerted him to the fact he'd overstepped his boundaries.

He eyed her for a moment. A kaleidoscope of emotions flitted across his features—suspicion, intrigue, and finally, concern. The interest in his gaze turned to tenderness. He leaned forward to close the gap between them.

"That was not a come-on, Ms. Connor, merely an observation. I'm a happily married man."

Tiny bubbles of hot air burst beneath her skin and scorched her cheeks. "I apologize for misunderstanding."

She held her breath and sent silent, fervent pleas for grace heavenward until he dropped his gaze to the plans once more. Thirty minutes later she left the office and drove to the nearest lumber yard to pick up tools she'd need to cultivate the lawn.

She perused the garden center and made a mental list of what plants and shrubs they had in stock. She also noted the faux rocks and boulders as well as stones and rough wood she could use in the design her employer chose.

Excitement paved the way to the home across town from where she and Laurel lived. She parked her car, climbed out, and leaned against the door for a moment.

Visions of new grass, green shrubs, and a stone walkway filled her mind. Instead of flowers, he'd have a rock garden. In place of roses, a barrel cut in half and filled with local wildflowers would suffuse the area around the front entry with scent and add a splash of color to the otherwise masculine decor.

Makes no sense to stand around and daydream about the end result, time to get to work and make it happen.

She slathered sunscreen on her bare arms and face, pulled on canvas work gloves, then slapped the cap on her head. She took the spade, shovel and rake out of the car, then set to work.

About mid-morning she sat on the porch, pulled a water bottle out of her lunch cooler, and took a sip. The refreshing liquid relieved her parched throat. She closed her eyes and took a deep breath. Contentment rolled through her. It had been so long... The smell of freshly turned earth. The vision of what would be...

The hours flew by. When her stomach growled Lorelei glanced at her watch in surprise and decided to go home for an hour or so, eat lunch, and rest, before tackling the afternoon chores.

The first thing she did when she got home was to shower off the dirt and grime from her activities. Her sandwich had wilted despite the coolness of the lunch bucket, so she prepared another and poured herself a tumbler of milk.

Carrying the plate and glass into the living room, she sat on the couch and propped her feet up on the coffee table. Before the first bite, she bowed her head.

"Lord, I'm forever amazed at Your provision. This job fits every desire of my heart – the pay, the hours, and the opportunity to beautify an otherwise bare lawn. And this town is so lovely, so beautiful and quaint. I feel Your presence everywhere I go. May Your glory reflect in everything I do and may we finally find a restful place to settle. In Jesus' name I pray. Thank You. Amen."

Peace reigned throughout her hour-and-a-half break, and she returned to finish the day's work with vigor.

****

Lorelei stretched beneath the cotton sheets and hummed with pleasure at the firmness of her bed and the clouds of softness surrounding her. Ever since her employer revealed who rented the log cabin where she currently worked, dreams of Carson Alexander haunted her thoughts. She closed her eyes and felt him beside her. Her arms ached to draw him close. Mouth watered for want of his kiss.

Her eyes snapped open. *Where on earth did*

that *come from?*

She recalled how cute he was, dressed in blue-jean shorts and sleeveless T shirt with his hair mussed from the wind the day he rode his bicycle to her house to discuss Laurel's writing assignment. And the following morning when he appeared at church adorned in sharp, well-pressed dress slacks, a polo shirt pulled tight across the broad expanse of his chest, and not a caramel-colored hair out of place, he took her breath away.

She flung the covers back, slid from the bed and willed her chattering pulse under control. Her mind continued to whirl around the man. Something about him pulled at her as no other had. Not even Laurel's father. She'd showered and changed into work clothes before she realized the thought of her ex-husband failed to stir unease in her heart.

She glanced at the clock. Time for one cup of coffee before Laurel had to rise and get ready for school. She moseyed into the kitchen and turned on the coffee pot. In a spur-of-the-moment decision, she whipped up a batch of lemon poppy-seed muffins and bacon for their breakfast.

Four hours later, she scraped the damp hair away from her face. The scent of rain hung heavy in the air. Heat and humidity stifled her creativity and drained her energy. She'd been on the job for more than two weeks but because her hours were scheduled around Laurel's day, she'd yet to actually meet up with Carson again.

Today, Laurel accompanied her. She woke up this morning and complained she didn't feel well so Lorelei allowed her to miss school and tag along. Her malady disappeared about midday and her daughter wandered off to explore the wooded area bordering the property.

Since whatever plagued the child seemed to fade as the day wore on, Lorelei decided to work as long as the weather held out.

Thunder rumbled in the distance. She straightened from her task of transplanting flowers into the barrel beside the front door, rolled her shoulders and called Laurel back to the house as dark billows continued to roll in from the south.

She raised her gaze skyward. "C'mon down rain, won't hurt my feelings a bit," she muttered at the water-laden clouds. "The plants and grass could use a good soaking, too."

As if on cue, lightning sliced the sky. Thunder roared, and the heavens opened up.

Lorelei tossed down the spade, stepped into the downpour and opened her arms wide to embrace the coolness. Within moments her clothes clung like a second skin. She brushed the drenched locks away from her face, undid the ponytail and shook out her hair.

She rolled the barrel out from under the protection of the porch so the flowers could relish the moisture and absorb the nourishment contained in the potting soil. Laurel joined her and they frolicked in the rain, dancing around the barrel. The next streak of electricity came a little too close for comfort.

"Under the porch, kiddo!"

She hurried to the car and took out the bags she always carried for emergencies or just in case they had to run again. One contained pajamas and a change of clothing for Laurel and herself, personal items, a small stash of cash, power candy bars, and two water bottles. The other held a couple of towels, washcloths, and toiletries in case they had to shower at a truck stop or rest area while traveling.

Laurel's father's face rose in Lorelei's mind. A shiver shook her entire being. "You won't scare me off this time. I'm tired of running."

Thunder rumbled like eerie laughter. Lightning crashed. Electricity along the power lines above her crackled. She all but jumped out of her skin. Terror gripped its icy fingers around her heart. She scampered back to the porch, dug out a towel for Laurel and one for herself.

She rubbed the thick terrycloth briskly to

erase the goose bumps that rose on her skin.

Laurel turned, her eyes wide with apprehension, as the wind howled around them. "What are we going to do?"

Lorelei brushed a hand over her daughter's hair. "As soon as the rain slacks off, we'll go home."

An SUV pulled into the drive and stopped alongside her car. They watched a man disembark, pull a jacket over his head, and run toward them. He hurled up the steps and skidded to a stop just shy of knocking them down. He muttered an apology, stripped off the jacket and shook it out while glancing in their direction. Surprise widened his eyes.

"Laurel, Ms. Connor. What are you two doing here?"

Before either could answer, thunder shattered the atmosphere like a blast of gunshot and lightning split the sky like a knife ripping through silk. Both shrieked. Laurel all but jumped into her mother's arms.

Carson felt a charge in the atmosphere. Electrical pulses pricked his spirit. Apprehension stiffened his spine. He noticed the hint of distress deep within Lorelei's gaze. "What is it?"

She blinked then frowned. "What's what?"

"Something's wrong. I can feel it. What

happened? Are you OK?"

"Nothing happened. The clap of thunder caught me off guard is all. I'm fine."

Carson reined in his emotions as the chaos around them increased. The wind wailed with an ominous moan. Rain pounded the earth in angry torrents. Lightning struck again, followed by a loud crash, as a tree grumbled and groaned, and then fell across both of their vehicles. A black streak ran up the trunk. Smoke curled in the air and the branches were in flames.

"Oh, God, my car!"

"Mom!" Laurel screamed, as Lorelei lunged toward the steps.

Carson caught her around the waist. "Lorelei, stop, we need to call nine-one-one!"

She struggled for a moment, her eyes wide with terror, panic etched in every feature. Then she glanced at Laurel, who quaked with fright as the elements continued to rage. She squared her shoulders and stepped over to embrace her daughter.

Carson dug his house key out of his pocket, unlocked the door and walked inside.

"Where are you going?" Laurel cried. "Please don't leave us out here all alone!"

He turned to reassure her, but Lorelei took the hysterical child's face in her hands and gave her a slight shake.

"It's OK, Laurel, look at me."

Carson moved to where they stood. "I'm going to call nine-one-one and get the camera. I'll be right out. Would you two like to come inside?" He waited until they crossed the threshold then followed them in and called the emergency number to report the incident.

"What do you need a camera for?" Laurel asked when he hung up the phone.

"We'll need pictures to file insurance claims on the cars." He turned to Lorelei. "You do have insurance, don't you?"

She nodded.

"Good." He walked into another room, fetched his digital camera, then went back out on the porch, and began taking pictures.

Laurel turned a turbulent gaze toward her mother.

"Isn't it dangerous for him to be doing that with all the lightening going on out there?"

Before Lorelei could respond, thunder boomed.

Laurel yelped and clung, sobs shaking her shoulders once more.

Lorelei wrapped her arms around her daughter and stroked her hair in a soothing gesture. "Sounds like the storm is lessening and moving away. Listen... One Mississippi. Two Mississippi."

Laurel quieted, and then counted the seconds with her to see how far the thunder and lightning had traveled, their voices barely above a whisper... "Three Mississippi. Four Mississippi."

Four miles.

The next clap echoed from even further across the distance. The wind died down a notch. The rain slowed to a steady patter on the metal roof. Thunder rumbled again, yet even farther away this time. Sirens rent the air. They moved to the window and watched as volunteer fire fighters, followed by the Sheriff, filled the yard.

Once they extinguished the flames, Carson and three firemen heaved the tree off the vehicles and rolled it out of the drive. Assured none of them were physically hurt, the people disappeared as fast as they had gathered.

"I'm going to go see how bad things are." Lorelei hurried outside. She grabbed the towel she'd used earlier and walked toward Carson, who braced himself against the hood of his SUV, covered in sweat and grime.

She reached his side and offered him a towel. Emotions roiled in her gut. *They could have been in that car!*

Tears filled her eyes, rolled down her cheeks. "What am I going to do now? That car is all I own in this world."

Carson heaved a sigh and brushed the cloth over his face. "I imagine we'll both need to call our insurance companies and then try to rent a car." He handed the towel back to her. "May I ask what you're doing here in the first place?"

She dried her eyes. "Mr. Flaven hired me to landscape your yard. Didn't he tell you?"

"He told me he'd hired someone, but not who. Now I understand why I saw evidence of work done, but never anyone working. You must come during school hours only."

Laurel's voice trembled behind them before she could respond. "Mom?"

Lorelei pulled her daughter close.

Carson smiled at the child. "I missed you in class today, Laurel."

"I wasn't feeling well so mom let me stay with her."

"Well, I hope it was nothing serious. Why don't we all go back inside and make those phone calls? We're not going anywhere soon, in either of these vehicles."

They walked back toward the house as the storm limped away, its fury spent.

Carson indicated the duffle bags on the porch. "I'm assuming these are yours?"

Lorelei nodded. "I grabbed them when the weather turned real nasty."

The moment he touched them his blood began to pound, vision blurred. Familiar sensations crawled up his spine. He tamped down on the beast within and lifted the bags. "You must have been a Girl Scout, always prepared."

A wary look crossed her face. Lorelei shrugged and averted her gaze.

"I learned when Laurel was a baby to keep a packed bag in the car."

Instinct and the way she avoided his eyes told Carson there was more to the story than that, but he bit back on his questions. He followed them into the house and called his insurance company while Lorelei and Laurel showered and changed into dry clothes.

He cleaned up while she phoned her insurance company then looked up the number to the only rental agency listed in the local phone directory. He dialed the number, surprised when someone actually answered, considering it was past five o'clock on a Friday afternoon.

"Rick's Rides."

"Yes, I need to speak to Rick about renting a couple of vehicles."

"Sorry but Rick is out of town. His twin sister Ruth had to have an emergency appendectomy and he needed to help his brother-in-law harvest the crops. I'm pretty sure he won't be back until Monday. Besides we only have three cars and two of them are out for the weekend. I can let you rent the one we have left if you can get here before six."

Carson glanced at his watch—five forty-five. "You don't pick up?"

She huffed. "No. We don't."

Her tone reeked of attitude. Heat rose in his veins. "Can you recommend another agency?"

"There's several over in Nashville."

His hand tightened on the receiver at the exasperation in her voice. He clenched his teeth and strove to keep a civil tongue. "Nashville is a half-hour away and I have no way to get there."

"Well, there might be one that picks you up," she quipped, with more than a hint of sarcasm.

He managed to mutter, "thank you," before slamming the phone back in its cradle.

He turned to Lorelei. "Looks like having a packed bag in the car is a pretty smart move. You might be stuck here for the night, or until Monday. Unless a car company in Nashville will drive out to pick us up—which I doubt they'll do this late. But maybe we can get a ride there tomorrow."

"I'm sorry we're such an imposition."

Heat suffused his face. He shook his head.

"You're not an imposition and I'm not frustrated at you, but the brat on the other end of the phone line. Trust me, I'll have a talk with Rick of 'Rick's Rides' when he returns. Don't know how the man stays in business with someone like that handling things while he's away."

He pulled a larger phone book out of the drawer and looked up the number to the car rental closest to them. That call confirmed his prediction. The company would drive out, but not until the next day.

"Well, what would you ladies like for dinner? I'm thinking spaghetti."

Laurel whooped. "I love spaghetti!"

Lorelei cackled. "Any and every kind. This child would live off that dish alone if I let her."

Carson slid his arm through Laurel's and then offered Lorelei his other arm. Slivers of delight coiled through him when she accepted. "My sentiments exactly. Spaghetti it is, then. Of course, there are the makings of a nice green salad. And if you have room for dessert, we can mix and bake a batch of brownies. I have whipped topping or ice cream to go with them."

An appreciative hum escaped both females. He led the way into the kitchen and waved them to a seat. The three of them chatted while he prepared the meal. When Lorelei offered, he enlisted their help in setting the table and pouring drinks. Tension slithered up his spine when, seated once more, each took one of his hands then bowed their heads and said grace.

"You don't say grace?" Laurel asked.

Her mother shushed her. "Don't be rude, Laurel. Some people aren't comfortable enough with God to say grace at every meal."

Laurel frowned. "But you always said being grateful for food is the least we can do to show appreciation for God's blessing and provision in our life."

"It's OK," Carson interrupted before Lorelei could correct her daughter again. "I don't say grace as often as I should, Laurel. Thank you for reminding me."

He turned to Lorelei. "So, you believe there's actually hope for my pathetic yard?" Her smile took his breath away.

"No place is hopeless. If you'd like we can walk around after dinner, and I'll explain what I plan to do."

"Sounds great. I'd love to hear your ideas. What about you and Laurel, what does the future hold for you two?"

Laurel's snort cut off her mother's reply. "I just wish we would settle in one place for longer than a school year."

Lorelei's cool, measured, look stopped further comments from her daughter. Awkward silence ensued. Carson scrambled for something to say to ease the friction that sprang up between his guests.

"So, Laurel, how do you like the spaghetti?"

Her face lit up. Her eyes danced. "There's something different in the way yours tastes. An odd but delicious flavor I haven't had before. What did you add that others don't?"

He grinned. "Old family recipe, classified. If I told you, then I'd have to kill you."

She giggled and his spirit leapt at the sound. Impressions swarmed his subconscious. Anguish pricked his heart. Moisture filled his gaze. *She doesn't laugh as a child should.*

He took a deep breath and excused himself. In the kitchen, he banged around while retrieving the items needed for dessert. "Lord, what are You showing me here? What is going on?"

A vision of green eyes wrought with pain, underscored with terror, and swimming with tears filled his mind. *But why?* He hoped to find the answer in ample time to prevent the tragedy he sensed lurking on the horizon.

After dinner and dessert, Carson made the bed in the spare room, while Lorelei and Laurel, cleaned the kitchen. He settled Laurel in front of the television, and handed her the remote, then he and Lorelei walked outside.

"Looks like you achieved quite a bit already."

She nodded. "Most of the grunt work is done. For the time being. The barrels of wildflowers will sit beside the door." She pointed to an area beneath his living room window.

"Instead of flowers there too, you'll have a rock garden with a couple of shrubs. A stone walkway will lead up to the porch steps. I'll build the outlines for both next week and, if possible, start the placement of stones. I'll pick up shrubs and transplant them later in the week.

"If the weather continues to hold out, I should finish the front within another week, two at the most. I'll start cultivating the back after that." She walked around the house, describing the work in store.

Carson tried to envision the end result of her landscape design but found he could hear nothing but the sound of her voice as it feathered over him, curling through his senses like a caress. Nor could he see past her animated features and the way her eyes lit up when she spoke.

"So, what do you think?"

"Beautiful," he whispered. He caressed her cheek, brushed his thumb across the soft curve of flesh. When she didn't bolt, he urged her closer and cupped her face in both hands, marveling at the texture of ivory skin beneath his fingers.

Emotions swarmed his heart and filled his spirit with light and color. Blood thundered through his veins. His mouth hovered over hers. A wary look flashed in her eyes. She stiffened and took a step back.

Carson felt the separation as acutely as he would a knife to the heart. He was shocked at his slide into sensuality – he barely knew the woman! She must think he was one of those men who looked for casual sex everywhere. But he wasn't. Never had been, even as a teen. He'd always been too wary, too cautious.

Why had he felt that soul-deep connection that made his body think she belonged to him? What was his heart trying to tell him?

"I'm sorry... I... can't."

He cocked his head, disoriented between his mixed emotions and the wary anxiety lurking deep within her emerald gaze. "Can't what?"

"Get involved with you."

"One kiss doesn't constitute involvement."

She turned on her heel and hurried into the house.

He watched her flee. Disturbing sensations shivered over him. He hesitated, struggled against the onslaught, then let the visions come.

Nothing concrete, only images and sensations. Violence. Fear. Desperation.

Exhausted, he retired to his room and stretched out on the bed. Fueled by dreams, sleep eluded him. A noise sounded from the kitchen. He jerked upright and glanced at the clock. Ten past midnight.

Rising, he went to investigate, surprised to find Lorelei puttering around. The sight of her sent his imagination into a tailspin. He watched her for a moment, his senses heightened, awareness tuned to the slightest change in environment. "Are you OK?"

She jumped at the sound of his voice. "Oh! I didn't hear you. Did I disturb you? I tried to be quiet."

He reached a hand to steady her. "You didn't disturb me. I couldn't sleep anyway."

A strained smile tilted the corners of her mouth. Her eyes filled with anxiety. Tears threatened. Carson reached out and stroked her hair, his touch gentle and meant to soothe.

A hint of warmth flickered in her eyes. She stepped forward, put her arms around his waist, and rested her cheek against his heart. When she pulled away, he let go.

His surprise was soul deep. Was she feeling the connection, too?

"I'm undecided if I want a cup of tea or hot

chocolate. What do you think?"

He smiled down at her. "Chocolate sounds wonderful. Laurel fast asleep?"

She giggled. "That child slumbers like the comatose through practically anything."

He laughed. "My nieces, nephews, and younger siblings can too. One of the blessings of youth, I guess."

She found one of his saucepans and poured milk into it. "How many brothers and sisters do you have?"

He retrieved the cocoa and handed it to her. "There are eight of us, total. I'm the oldest boy but have three older sisters and four younger brothers."

She stirred in chocolate. "Wow. It must be nice to come from such a large family. I'm an only child. Orphaned at seventeen.

She tested the temperature of the milk with her finger. An innocent gesture on her part, but it had the same effect on him as a kick to the solar plexus. He swallowed hard and tried to focus on the conversation at hand. "Sorry to hear that. What happened?"

Emotions clouded her gaze. "Drunk driver."

He took two mugs out of the cabinet and placed them on the counter. She filled them with the warm brew then handed him one. Their hands brushed. Awareness tingled between them. His mind careened. Impressions bombarded his system. Alarm raced over his nerve endings. His eyes narrowed, breath heaved out in uneven pants. Sweat popped out on his forehead and upper lip.

"Carson, are you all right?"

Her voice, rippled with tension, rang in his ears.

"He's close."

She hissed in a sharp breath. "What? Who's close?"

He shook his head, swallowed hard. He scraped the heels of his hands over his eyes and down his face, felt the blood drain from his features.

"Your ex-husband. Was he abusive to you, brutal?"

She frowned. "How do you know this?"

"He's deranged. You and Laurel are in danger this time."

She whirled away. "OK, now I'm freaked. How do you know these things?"

Carson saw the apprehension on her face and took a mental and physical step back. *God help me reach her. Make her understand!*

Although she'd stepped back, she hadn't run. Did she have some experience with his talent? He grasped the counter behind him, locked gazes with her, and prepared for the usual reaction to his next words. "Do you believe in prophetic or psychic abilities?"

An array of emotions clouded her eyes— a hint of concern and a glimmer of doubt shadowed by a tinge of mockery. She looked at him for a long, tense moment, then cleared her throat. "The media is bombarded with so called prophets and psychics."

He conceded her statement with a slight incline of his head. "I know that. But do *you* believe in them?"

"Not sure how much I believe. The Bible speaks of prophets and at the same time, warns us not to deal with mediums or sorcerers. I try to abide by that. I may glance at my horoscope from time to time, but I don't put much store in what it says. Laurel and I both get a kick out of fortune cookies, but other than those, or palm readers and such at carnivals, which we all know is a farce, I've never had any dealings with one."

He held a hand toward her, the ultimate test. "Let's sit and talk."

She took a step back, hesitated a moment, then agreed with a slight inclination of her head.

His lips curved in a tentative gesture. "Chocolate's probably cold by now. Want me to warm it in the microwave?"

"Sure."

Lorelei pulled out a chair, waited for him to

join her. Scriptures which spoke of prophets intermingled with those against witchcraft and sorcery circled in her mind. Dread tightened her lungs. Silent prayers rose with each ragged breath. The microwave beeped and she nearly bolted.

Carson set down her cup of chocolate then sat. She wrapped both hands around the hot mug in hopes the tremors would cease but dared not lift the cup to her mouth lest she spill its contents.

"You look terrified."

He sounded normal, but she wondered about his sanity. "Not every day one meets a psychic."

He scoffed. "Or a psycho?"

Heat climbed up her neck, stung her cheeks. She refrained from commenting.

He lifted his cup with a shaky hand, took a sip, grimaced, then set it on the table with a soft thud. "I don't even know where to start."

"What makes you say you're psychic or prophetic?"

"Guess I've always known. Even as a young boy I knew things. Most of the time fun things like where someone hid, or what color shirt they'd have on, or what shoes my sisters would wear. As I got older, my abilities sharpened. I started having premonitions, many of which came true. At first, I assumed everyone has this power but soon learned that's not only untrue, but many are afraid of those of us who do. I learned to keep the impressions to myself or make light of it when I predicted something, and the event occurred."

A bitter little laugh escaped his humorless smile.

"Folks tend to shy away or worse, get nasty. This aptitude, deemed both a curse and a gift, has labeled me a warlock or freak. Even a heretic. Especially when I say God has shown or told me something."

Lorelei's heart cringed at the anguish in his eyes. "Regardless of the origin of their faith or level of belief, many are afraid of the supernatural."

He chewed on his bottom lip. His voice lowered a notch when he continued. "I don't understand how people can claim to know God and yet, mock His anointed ones. I was raised in the church, known Him all my life, did my best to honor and respect Him in everything."

"I'm sure you did and continue to do so, Carson, but you must consider the countless numbers of those who do the opposite. How does your family feel about this?"

He blinked hard and set his jaw. His struggle for composure tugged at her heartstrings.

"My family…" He cleared his throat, swallowed hard. "They supported me until our parents died. Then they blamed me. Said I could have done more to stop Mom and Dad. Only one sister and my brothers seem to understand. Or at least they've forgiven my failure."

"Could you have stopped them?"

His eyes swam with emotions.

"I tried. I told them everything I knew, all I felt. My parents, devout Catholics, were… I wouldn't say doubtful or ashamed but perplexed by my abilities. They never shunned me or shamed me into keeping quiet, but I don't think they believed wholeheartedly. Both were quick to defend me to others when cornered or questioned…" He trailed off, swallowed hard again.

The anguish in his voice sluiced through the doubt in her mind. "This has caused a breach in your relationship with more than your family, hasn't it? You've struggled with God over it, haven't you?"

"What's the use of this ability if nobody listens?"

"I don't know, but I'm sure God has a plan."

"Yeah, I thought so, too. Once upon a time, but not anymore. I wish He'd just take it back."

"Be careful what you wish for. He may take

back the gift, but who will that benefit?"

His eyes bored into hers. "So, you believe me? What would you say if I told you I think you and Laurel should move in with me? To be safe from him."

Lorelei searched her heart and chose her words with care. "I believe you have this ability, and I'm sure you mean well. But I can't simply pack my daughter up and move in with you. What will people think? Especially those with whom we attend church."

"Then marry me. I can't keep you safe if I'm not around when he shows up."

She gaped at him. "You barely know me!"

"In the natural, yes," He touched his chest. "But something in here knows you. God, my heart, something. Tell me you don't feel a connection."

She stared at him, wanting, but unable to deny his words in her heart. Finally, she spoke again. "I'll do whatever it takes to protect myself and Laurel. But you can't keep watch over us all the time either. You teach. Laurel has school, and I have work.

"Unless we are all together twenty-four-seven, which is impossible, we've got to figure out a plan. I'm not going to marry you out of fear and desperation. There has to be another way."

Silence stretched. Trepidation shimmered

up her spine. She picked both mugs of cold chocolate, carried them to the sink, dumped the contents and turned on the hot water. A swish of soap and a quick rinse under the scalding tap and she placed them in the drain board. Something resonated in his words, though.

Marriage. Family.

Carson's chair scraped back from the table. His footsteps moved soft but sure in her direction. She turned to face him. The tenderness in his eyes battered her control. Gentle hands encased her waist. She buried her face against his chest, relished the strong, solid feel of his arms around her and his hands stroking her hair. He brushed his lips over her head.

"We'll figure it out."

Her heart beat double-time at the husky tone of his voice. *Funny how safe, and secure, she felt in his arms. This man she barely knew.*

She let him lead her into the living area and cuddled with him on the couch. Quiet conversation flowed between them into the wee hours of the morning.

****

Dawn broke in an amazing display of light and color. The dark fury of yesterday's storm seemed surreal against the brilliance of morning. Carson shifted Lorelei out of his embrace. He pulled the afghan off the back of the couch and covered her.

Under a hot shower, he worked the kinks out of his back, neck, and shoulders. Familiar sensations curled up his spine. He hesitated in his task, bent his head under the pulsating spray then let the visions come. Again, nothing concrete, only vague inklings of dread and the lingering taste of terror.

Lord, I know we're not on the best speaking terms but You're going to have to give me more this time. My heart is already bound by this woman and her child. I couldn't bear to lose someone I care about again.

The images stopped. His emotions untangled. Peace reigned in their wake. He breathed a sigh of relief and finished showering. He dressed, then exited his bedroom and bumped into Laurel as she stumbled out of the guest room. "Whoa there, you OK?"

She rubbed her eyes and mumbled, "Mom's not in bed."

"She's on the couch. We were up quite late, so let's not disturb her. OK?"

She nodded.

"Hungry?"

"Starved."

He grinned. "There's cereal and pastries in the kitchen. Make yourself at home. I'm going to ride my bike into town and rent whatever vehicle they have left. Once I return, I'll drive you and your mom to Nashville to rent something."

They headed in opposite directions. He rode to Rick's Rides, thrilled to find he didn't have to deal with the same snotty girl who answered the phone last night, although he did voice his complaint. An hour-and-a-half later, he returned to find Laurel in front of the television. A kid's station blared out of the tube. Lorelei nursed a cup of coffee on the couch. He held a hand toward her. "Coffee smells wonderful. Got another cup?"

Lorelei allowed him to lead her into the kitchen.

He lowered his lips close to her ear and whispered, "Even wrinkled from sleep you're beautiful."

His husky voice made her heart flutter, nerves quiver. He chuckled. Heat filled her cheeks then spread like a warm glow. She elbowed him in the abdomen and grinned at his soft grunt. "Behave yourself."

"Shucks. Can't have any fun, even in my own house."

Her lips bowed in response to the pouty lilt

in his voice.

He caressed her cheek. "Now that's worth an elbow to the gut any day."

"You are an incurable tease, Carson Alexander."

He glanced over his shoulder. Her gaze followed his to make sure Laurel still sat glued to the television. Their eyes locked in a heated embrace. He boxed her in against the counter, brushed his lips across hers, lingered a moment, then stepped back.

"No teasing here, sweetheart. I'm as serious as a heartbeat. You captivated me the moment you stepped out of your dollhouse with your back up and eyes flashing, ready to defend your daughter against her nosy English teacher."

He walked over to the table, pulled out a chair, and waited while she sank into it.

"I'll pour us a cup and join you in a jiffy."

She mumbled her thanks, took a deep breath, and willed her flighty pulse into some semblance of normal.

What on earth is wrong with you? The silent question screamed through her brain.

I've never felt this way before, her heart answered. *There's just something about him and it's more than looks.* The thought curved her lips.

Carson set a cup in front of her. "You have a

beautiful smile."

His husky voice caressed her senses. She turned that smile on him, watched the corners of his mouth curl in response. Her heart catapulted at the warm, slightly wicked gleam in his eyes. He moved to the chair across from her, placed his cup on the table, and sat down. Her hand slid over his. Her pulse leapt into high gear when he turned his hand palm up and interlocked his fingers with hers.

Physical attraction mellowed and anchored their hearts into peace and purpose. "I know we need a plan, but I don't want Laurel to know what's going on."

He eyed her with more than a hint of curiosity. "With me, us, or your ex?"

"None of the above."

He arched an eyebrow. Irritation flitted over his features. A hint of doubt and pain darkened his gaze and tugged at her heart. She squeezed his hand. "You're her teacher and I don't want her to feel pressured, or insecure, or any of the numerous negative emotions that will certainly come with the knowledge of us as a couple. Nor do I want her to be afraid or intimidated by your gift."

She waited a beat, took a sip of coffee, and then continued. "I promised her this would be our last move, and I refuse to be goaded into running again. She needs a home and stability. I haven't been able to give her that. I want to now."

He lifted their clasped hands, brushed his lips over her knuckles. "Makes perfect sense."

His gaze sharpened. Goose bumps rose on her arms. The hair on the back of her neck stood on end. Her heart began to shudder. She jerked her hand back, curled both fists into her lap. "What?"

He leaned forward in his chair; his intense gaze lit from within. "I feel like I should know him. What's his name?"

"Jaxon Devereaux."

He reared back as though slapped, a stunned expression on his face. His breath heaved in and out in harsh pants. "Oh, my God." He rolled his eyes heavenward. "You've got to be kidding, Lord."

Lorelei didn't know if the words were a prayer or curse. She remained silent.

"My sister..." His words faded into silence.

He shook his head, shock evident in his tone and the paleness of his skin. Tension slithered through the atmosphere and settled between them. Desperate to be voiced aloud, the question hung in the air like a noxious cloud. Lorelei clenched her hands into fists and blurted out the words. "Who is your sister?"

"Julia Alexander Devereaux."

She felt the blood drain from her limbs. Her breath trapped in her lungs. Shock collided with horror and propelled her into action. She sprang from the chair and glared. "What kind of sick joke is this?"

"No joke."

She stepped back and called out to Laurel. "Get dressed, we're leaving."

Laurel protested.

Her eyes narrowed and she stormed into the living room. "Don't question or argue with me, young lady. Just do as I say."

He rose as Laurel scurried from the room. "Lorelei, wait."

She turned on him in an angry whirl. "You stay away from us."

He strode into the living room and led her back into the kitchen. "Calm down."

She stiffened and jerked free from his grasp. "Call me a cab."

"I'll drive you to rent a car. But you've got to calm down. There's a reason God brought you here, and us together. Lorelei, please, think about this. It's possible I'm the only one who can protect you and Laurel."

Her gaze searched his. Tears sprang to life, spilled down her cheeks. "I swear I didn't know he was married. I *never* would have had anything to do with a married man much less marry him myself. He never mentioned a wife or even an ex-wife for that matter. He simply waltzed into my life right after my parents died, sweet talked his way through my grief, and took advantage of my naiveté and innocence."

Her voice quivered. She rubbed her eyes and continued. "When I found out he was married, which made our union illegal and Laurel illegitimate, I left. He's followed me ever since, wants to take Laurel away from me. I'll die before I let him."

Carson cradled her face and brushed the moisture off her cheeks with his thumbs. "I believe you, sweetheart. You weren't the first in a long string of affairs and abuse directed toward Julie from this psycho. She couldn't have children, and when she found out about Laurel after a beating, that added insult to injury. They've been divorced for more than seven years now. I'm grateful you got away before he hurt you as badly, or worse than he hurt her."

She shook her head, stepped away. "I need to think, to plan. I can't do that here."

He nodded. "I understand but promise you won't do anything rash. Promise you won't run. I can't protect you if I don't know where you are."

She stood, transfixed by his steady gaze.

Calmed by the strength reflected in his eyes. Her heart, her traitorous heart, filled with warmth, steady as his gaze. "I promise."

****

Carson took Lorelei and Laurel into Nashville to rent a vehicle then drove home in a fog. Confusion battled with trepidation. Fear left a metallic taste in his mouth. His clenched fist banged on the steering wheel. "God, I wish you hadn't done this to me again! Five years of peace and now this!"

Peace?

The question echoed in his mind. Not really, he conceded. Avoidance maybe, but no peace.

For five years he ignored the call on his life, avoided extraneous contact with people, and stuffed everything deep inside. Including his faith. None of those efforts brought him true peace or a hint of happiness. He did have a bit of solitude and a lot of loneliness, but little joy, and no purpose.

Now, when he finally decided to try and rebuild at least a small measure of what he had before, this *thing* starts up again. And it apparently came to life when he opened his heart to really care about someone! He arrived home, barreled out of the car, and raised his fist to the sky.

"You cost me everything with this... this... curse! Why can't I just be normal?"

"It shall come to pass, that I will pour out my Spirit upon all flesh; and your sons and your daughters shall prophesy, your old men shall dream dreams, your young men shall see visions..."

He slumped down on the steps with a moan. "Why me?"

"Because you were dedicated to me the day you were born."

The answer shocked him. Dedicated? What on earth did that mean? His parents were Catholic—they didn't dedicate babies, they christened them. He'd followed the rules and regulations of his religion... First Reconciliation, then Communion, and as a teen, Confirmation. He hadn't strayed from Catholicism until college when he studied religion as an elective. So, when did this dedication taken place?

Only one way to find out.

He pulled his cell phone from the front pocket of his slacks, flipped it open and dialed his parent's house. His sister Julie, the youngest of three girls, and closest to his age, answered.

"Hello?"

"Hey, Jules. How are you?"

"Carson? Hey! It's been so long. How are

you?"

"I'm OK, Jules. Miss you all. How are the boys?"

"Good. Doug and Kyle are in their last semester at college. The twins are doing well in high school. The sisters and their broods are fine, too. What's up with you?"

"The impressions are back, Julie. In full force. I thought they were done with after the accident. Evidently God decided to give me a break is all. But the break is over. When I asked why me, He said I was dedicated to Him before I was born. Do you know anything about that?"

Her sigh spoke volumes. Carson heard her pull out a chair and plop down in it.

"You know how for years mom and dad prayed for a son, but she kept having miscarriages and all sorts of problems? While doing a Bible study, she came across the story of Hannah and how she prayed for a son and vowed to give him back to the Lord. She began to pray as Hannah prayed.

"When you came along, she told the priest about her prayer, so, not only were you christened, but you were also dedicated to the Lord for His service. We always figured that meant you'd become a priest or go into some type of ministry, especially when you started studying religion and theology in college. We never dreamed you would have the gift of prophesy."

"Or what it would cost."

"Cars..." She bit back the familiar argument. "When did the impressions start up again?"

"The first day of school."

"Something with a student, then. Boy or girl?"

"Girl."

"What's her name?"

"Laurel Connor."

"Hmm, sounds familiar."

There was no easy way soften the blow of his next words, but Carson tried. "Jules, she's Jaxon's child."

She gasped. "You're joking, right?"

Her voice held all the warmth of a glacier. The jagged shards pierced his heart. "Not at all. She's a beautiful girl, and her mother is amazing."

Julie snorted. "And you're in love with her. I can hear it in your tone. How could you fall for someone like that?"

"She didn't know he was married."

"So, *she* says."

Carson knew his sister's forgiving nature wouldn't allow her to stay angry long, especially if she knew the truth. "She was seventeen, Julie, and her parents were killed by a drunk driver.

"You know what a smooth talker Jaxon is. Once she found out he was bigamous, she left and took Laurel with her. He's stalked her ever since. I'm really worried this time. I believe Jaxon has crossed over the edge."

A tense silence stretched between them. Carson could all but hear the gears turn in Julie's mind and the echo of prayer from her heart. A deep exhale preceded her words.

"Be careful, Carson. Both of you be very careful and protect that child. I'll be praying. Meanwhile, if you need anything, holler. And please consider coming home for a visit."

"I will, Jules."

They said goodbye. Carson flipped the cell phone closed, slipped it in his pocket, then grabbed his keys and escaped to the cool, dark, recesses of his house.

That evening, he lay on his bed, hands clasped behind his head, every sensory receptacle in his body in full alert. Lorelei's reaction that morning to his sister's name, and Julie to hers, weighed on his mind and heart.

The fact that he had not heard from Lorelei since he dropped her, and Laurel, off at the car rental place, only enhanced the uneasiness he felt. He picked up the phone, dialed her number. The breath lodged in his chest escaped in a relieved sigh when she answered.

"You're still here."

"I told you already, I promised Laurel we'd settle here. And I assured you I wouldn't do anything rash. Don't you trust me to keep my word?"

"Of course, I do. Guess I'm feeling the strain of the last couple of days. How is Laurel?"

"Fine, clueless. At least I hope she's clueless. The child is exceptionally perceptive. She asked me what we were fighting about. I brushed her off with some lame explanation of grown-up stuff."

"What did she say?"

"She rolled her eyes and grunted, then went on about her business."

The humor in her voice warmed his heart, sent an ache through his entire being. "Are you sure you two can't move in over here?"

Heat curled over the line. Her sharp intake of breath assured him she felt it, too.

"Positive. And if you're going to start in on me about that, I'll hang up."

The husky, breathless sound of her voice made his body tighten with need. "Don't hang up. I'll behave."

"What do you want to talk about?"

"Doesn't matter as long as I can hear your voice."

Her heavy sigh curled through him,

quickened his pulse.

"How can it be we feel so much, and these feelings run so deep?"

"I don't know. But I'm not going to question what is obviously a rare and precious gift. Do you and Laurel plan to attend church tomorrow?"

"We do."

"Want to ride together, then grab some lunch?"

"Sounds fun."

"OK. I'll pick you two up around nine."

"Would you like to have breakfast with us?"

"I'd love to."

"OK. We'll see you around eight, then."

Her silence signaled the end of their conversation.

"Guess it's good night."

"'Night."

Carson fumbled to place the phone in its cradle. He awoke early the next morning, groggy and heavy-headed. Stumbling to the shower, he turned on the water, and stood a long time beneath the hot, pulsating spray. Her presence permeated his every pore as though they were one. His heart leapt. Body responded.

"Jesus. You'll have to get this physical thing out of the way if I'm to keep a level head about the situation."

The hot water stopped. He grimaced. *Nothing like a cold shower, right, Lord?*

Carson stepped from the tub, tied the towel around his waist, and moved to the sink to shave. Images of fear and violence reflected in the foggy mirror.

Jaxon's face, twisted with insanity, hovered over Lorelei and Laurel. His sadistic laughter echoed through the room.

Scripture reverberated through the atmosphere... *Be sober and vigilant because your adversary the devil roams about like a roaring lion, seeking whom he may devour.*

"Fear not for I am with you always, even unto the end," sounded clearly in the Voice he knew so well.

Carson stripped the towel from around his waist and wiped the glass clean. His hand shook when he applied a thick layer of shaving cream to his jaw. Turning on the tap, he jolted when hot water spewed from the spout. He swished the razor beneath the steamy stream then swept it upward along his jaw. Prayer poured from his heart with each swipe of the blade across his face.

"You know my heart, Lord, despite my anger. Equip me for the battle ahead. Allow me to redeem myself by protecting them."

Thirty minutes later, he knocked on

Lorelei's door. His heartbeat kicked into high gear. Her thick sable hair, clipped at the crown with a butterfly clasp, hung in soft curls over her shoulders and down her back. A cream-colored t-shirt dress, with bold green designs, brought out the golden flecks in her emerald eyes.

He glanced over her shoulder to see if Laurel stood nearby. Assured the coast was clear, he slid his hand around her waist, and, with a gentle tug, pulled the door shut behind her.

"God, you're beautiful." His lips brushed over hers in a tender gesture. Her arms crept around his neck. He clung to the doorknob with one hand to ensure Laurel would not catch them. His mouth swooped over hers, molded and clung, until each ragged breath she took robbed him of much needed oxygen. He ended the kiss by slow degrees, but held fast to the doorknob, and her, until she steadied in his grasp.

Parting was actually painful.

Lorelei leaned against the hard wooden structure. Her breath came sharp and severe. Her body ached from the strength of their embrace and yet, trembled with such violence her teeth threatened to chatter. "Carson, this has to stop."

He shook his head as though to clear his thoughts. "I prayed this morning for God to temper this physical reaction so I can stay focused on your and Laurel's safety. What I feel is more than physical, Lore, its soul deep."

"How can that be? We hardly know each other."

He shook his head again, caring etched in every feature, his eyes alive with emotions. "I don't know, but I refuse to discount this. Let's embrace what we feel, and the possibilities open to us."

Laurel's voice calling for her echoed.

Carson ran his knuckles along the curve of her cheek. The caress shivered through her entire being.

"You promised me breakfast."

His quick smile eased the tension sizzling between them. Her heart did a little jig then spiraled into her stomach where it settled with a happy flip and a warm tingle.

Laurel called again.

Lorelei turned, opened the door, and allowed his entrance. "Breakfast is coming right up."

She paused on her way to the kitchen to kiss her daughter and bid her good morning.

"What were y'all doing on the porch?"

"Talking."

Her eyes narrowed and gaze cut to Carson. "Are you two, like, dating or something?"

Carson raised a brow. "Exceptionally perceptive you said?"

Lorelei sent him a warning glare then turned back to her daughter. "Would that be so bad?"

Her face scrunched up. "Eeewwwee, he's my teacher."

"The best teacher in the whole world and you like him."

Laurel's face colored at being reminded of her words. "Yeah, but as a *teacher*. What will everybody at school say?"

Lorelei smiled and brushed the consternation off her daughter's face with a tender caress, then gave her a hug. "I like him too. As your teacher and as a man. But don't worry, if we start to like each other, as more than friends and parent/teacher, we'll be very discreet. Now, how about pancakes and bacon for breakfast?" she asked, and with the skill bestowed on all parents, turned her child's mind to more pressing matters—namely, her stomach.

"Great, I'm starved! I can't find my gold barrette."

"Think about the last time you wore it and I'm sure you'll figure out where you left it."

"Check under your bed," Carson interjected when Laurel headed out of the room.

Her excited yelp a moment later made them smile.

She rushed back into the room, fastening the clip in her hair. "Wow, are you psychic or something?"

He laughed. "Or something. I'm hungry too."

Carson sipped a cup of coffee and Laurel set the table while Lorelei prepared the meal. They ate breakfast, then piled up in the SUV he rented the day before and went to church. The morning passed without incident, as did lunch. In what appeared to be a spur-of-the-moment decision, they spent the afternoon watching movies and snacking on popcorn and candy.

Evening rolled around and though Laurel claimed to be ravenous, Carson and Lorelei were too full to contemplate more than soup and salad at a nearby diner. Night settled around them in various shades. Light from a full moon hung on a backdrop of black velvet, inset with a vast number of stars illuminating the darkness.

Carson bid them goodnight and left. Lorelei tucked Laurel into bed with a kiss on the cheek.

"Mr. Alexander really is a nice guy. Isn't he, Mom?"

Lorelei sat beside her daughter. "Yes, very nice."

"And you like him?"

"Very much so."

"Do you think he can protect us if Daddy shows up?"

"What makes you think your father will find us here?"

She shrugged. "Just a feeling."

Unease crept up her spine. Could it be her daughter and Carson shared a similar connection to God and the universe? "You get these 'feelings' often, Laurel?"

She squirmed. "Sometimes it's like I know something before it happens. Is that weird or what?"

Lorelei chose her words with care. "We are all spiritual beings, Laurel, living in a physical world. Some people retain their connection to the spiritual realm on a different level than others. There is nothing weird about that. In fact, I'd say the ability to discern things is a rare but precious gift from God. And, as long as you use that gift for good, and not evil, He will bless you and allow you to keep it."

"Mr. Alexander has the gift too, doesn't he?"

Lorelei stared at her daughter in consternation.

"I... I always know. There was this girl when I was in second grade and another teacher in fourth grade. I... We can feel it in each other when we get to know... at least, I think we can. I can. I usually ignore it unless I... Unless the Voice says something important.”

Lorelei raised her brows. “What would be important?

“Like if a ball is coming towards someone and it might hit them in the head. I yell watch out. But sometimes the ball hasn’t even been thrown yet.”

“I see.” Lorelei pulled the covers up over her girl. “I think Mr. Alexander might.”

“And you do like him, as more than a friend, don’t you? Be honest, now.”

Again, Lorelei chose her words with care. “I find myself drawn to him. Where that may lead is anybody’s guess. Since we’re being honest, how would you feel about that?”

Laurel’s face pinkened. Her eyes glowed. Her voice dropped to a shy tone. “I think he’s really neat and would make a great dad.”

“Do you feel safe and secure around him?”

Laurel nodded.

Lorelei hugged her. “So do I.” She rose and tucked the covers tighter around her daughter. “OK, enough talk. Time for bed. We have a full day tomorrow.”

“Will you be working at Mr. Alexander’s tomorrow?”

“Yes, and every day until I’m done.”

“Good. Love you, Mom.”

"I love you too, sweetheart."

Lorelei went into her bedroom and readied for sleep. All the while, questions rolled around in her head. Would Jaxon find them? Would Carson be able to protect her and Laurel if, *when* he did? Should she marry Carson? Would their relationship withstand whatever Jaxon had in mind? Did they even have a relationship?

She tossed and turned and at some point, fell into a restless slumber. Hours later she awoke drenched in sweat, her heart at a gallop, and her senses in full alert.

Laurel cried out.

Lorelei lunged from the bed and raced into her daughter's room. Laurel lay curled into a fetal position, a thumb in her mouth, and tears on her cheeks. Lorelei brushed the hair off her face, softly called her name. She whimpered.

Lorelei crawled under the covers, curled herself around her child, and whispered words of faith and comfort in an attempt to coax her from the place of terror in which she'd drifted while asleep. She awoke the next morning in a tangle of limbs and covers.

Careful not to wake Laurel, she slid from the bed, stumbled into the kitchen, and turned on the coffee pot. Her mind drifted back over the years and many times they'd run.

A pattern began to unfold when she realized

Laurel's actions last night emulated many before. Most of those times occurred on the eve of her decision to pack up and move.

Agony clenched her heart. *Had she caused fear to take root in her daughter's subconscious?*

Or could it be something else?

Could it be her decision to pack up and move was based on a gut instinct to protect her child when Laurel acted like this? Could Laurel's dreams be an indication Jaxon was near?

Goosebumps raced across her skin. The hair at the base of her neck prickled. A shiver shook her soul. She picked up the phone and dialed Carson's number.

"We need to talk."

The thread of tension in her voice set his teeth on edge. Carson gripped the phone, held it tighter against his ear. "What's wrong?"

"I think you were right, Saturday. I believe Jaxon is close."

"How do you know?"

What she revealed made his blood run cold. Her words left no doubt in his mind Laurel's spirit was sensitive.

"I don't know what to do."

Worry echoed in the words.

"I already told you what we should do."

"I will not marry you, and I certainly will not

live in sin with you."

The indignation in her voice made him chortle.

"Are you *laughing?*"

He managed to swallow the mirth and forced a measure of solemnity into his voice. "Only at your tone of voice, honey. Since you refuse to be sensible and marry me and you're determined not to run this time, what do you suggest?"

Her heavy sigh spoke volumes. "For starters, Laurel will not walk to or from school again. Nor will she be alone, for even a second, when not at school."

"Good. I don't like the idea of you at my place alone, either. Maybe we should talk to Mr. Flaven about putting off the landscaping until this is resolved."

"I'm not afraid for myself. It's Laurel he wants. Besides, I always have a shovel or something handy."

"That's good. Stay focused and alert. Keep your eyes and ears open. Always, Lorelei." He waited a beat to make sure his words had time to sink in then continued. "I think we should talk to the principal, and school counselor, and maybe the Sheriff."

"Do you really think all that is necessary?"

"If you intend to settle down here and not

ever run again, I do. Those in authority should know what's going on. That way, if Jaxon were to show up, they wouldn't let him see her. And if something happens, to him or one of us, the law would already be aware of the situation and be able to respond accordingly."

"I guess you're right. Can you set it up?"

"Sure."

"OK. I hear Laurel moving about so let me get in there and check on her. Depending on how she feels, we'll see you at school in a little while, or at your house. I'm not forcing her to go to school if she's not up to it."

"Understood."

They rang off. Carson poured another cup of coffee and pulled his Bible out of the drawer where it had rested, virtually untouched, for five years. Setting the heavy leather volume on the table he bowed his head. "OK, Lord, I surrender. You've given me this gift for a reason and I'm trying to come to grips with that despite the pain it's caused in my life. Give me discernment and wisdom that I do not fail again."

He rifled through the pages then let the Bible open to where it may. His eyes fell upon Samuel 2:3: *"Talk no more so very proudly; Let no arrogance come from your mouth, for the LORD is the God of knowledge; And by Him actions are weighed."*

Other scriptures on pride reverberated through his mind. The error of his ways became achingly clear. Though he sought to serve the Lord with his abilities, now he realized that, in the past, he'd often approached the people involved with an air of arrogance, thereby hindering the effect of the knowledge he'd received.

Insight and direction wove through the passages of scripture as did revelation. Conviction whispered. Guilt crushed. Repentance cleansed.

Never again, Lord, he vowed. *From this moment on I'll let You lead with Your heart through me.*

A vision rose in his mind—a German Shepherd, an animal born of strength and beauty. A dog bred to be docile yet fiercely loyal and well able to protect. A picture of Jesus carrying a lamb across his shoulders flashed in his mind, confirming the vision. He dressed for work and headed to the kennel in a neighboring town. The owner met him on the porch moments after he arrived.

"Can I help you?"

"I'd like to look at your Shepherds."

"Anything in particular you're looking for?"

"I need one young enough to bond, yet old and strong enough to protect."

The man hummed. "Well, I got this one dog. She's really good with kids. House broke and knows a few basic commands. She's well mannered, smart, gentle, and practically docile. Unless threatened."

He paused outside the last kennel in his enclosure but didn't open the door. "Only problem is, she ain't registered. She was given to me by some folks who moved last month. I have no idea of her bloodline, but I can tell you she's ninety-nine-percent pure. She's spayed and her shots are up to date."

"I don't care if she's registered or pure for that matter. The fact that she's good with kids and docile is perfect. How do you know she's aggressive when threatened?"

"When the folks that gave her to me brought her over, their young daughter dashed to the fence. One of my stud dogs ran toward her. He wouldn't have hurt her either mind you, but Princess here didn't know that. She hit that fence and all I saw was teeth and fur." He chortled at the memory.

"Every hair on her back and neck stood straight up and she snarled something fierce. I guarantee if he'd have gotten out, she would have torn him up. Or died trying. Want to take a look at her?"

Carson nodded and the man opened the

door and called the dog. "Princess, come here girl!"

One look at the slick, slender, juvenile female and Carson's heart cinched with confidence. This dog would fight to the death to defend the women he loved. "How much?"

"Well, I got about a hundred in her with vet bills. Give me that and I'll throw in enough food to last a day or two."

Carson paid the man then loaded Princess and the food into the SUV he'd rented. He called Lorelei and asked her to meet him at his house. In the course of conversation, he found she'd decided to keep Laurel with her for the day. *Perfect.*

He pulled into his driveway moments before Lorelei and Laurel arrived. When they disembarked and walked in his direction, he climbed out of the driver's seat, strolled around to the back of the vehicle, and opened the hatch. Princess sat up and crouched as though to jump out.

"No," Carson said, his voice firm.

The dog sat.

He palmed her head. "Good girl."

He scratched her under the chin then hooked the leash onto her collar, stepped back and snapped his fingers. "Come."

She jumped out of the vehicle.

"Sit." She promptly obeyed. Again, he ran his hand over her head and praised her good behavior. A delighted squeal from Laurel made him smile. At the sight of the young girl, Princess whimpered and whined. Though she held herself in control awaiting his command, her whole body quaked with joy and Carson knew he'd chosen wisely.

One glance at Lorelei and he sensed her approval. He stepped aside and unsnapped the leash. "Go."

The dog leapt into Laurel's arms and the two tumbled to the ground and rolled around in mutual admiration.

"Why don't you take her inside, Laurel, and find some bowls for her food and water for today. I'll pick up supplies on my way home this afternoon." When Laurel rose to do as he asked, with Princess in tow, he turned to Lorelei.

"She's house broken and trained to obey basic commands—sit, stay, no, heel, and go. You shouldn't have any trouble with her."

"She is certainly beautiful. Laurel's always wanted a dog, but I never got around to buying or adopting one."

"So, you don't mind?"

The smile she bestowed on him would have melted a glacier. Instead of an answer, she slid one hand around his neck, placed her other palm on his cheek and guided his lips toward hers. Her eyes widened, pupils darkened and dilated. Her breath caught in an audible gasp. Lips parted. Her soft hum shivered through him.

A simple shift and they were torso to torso. His hands roamed over her shoulders, stroked her back. He slid deeper into the kiss, savored the texture, and tasted the honeyed sweetness of her mouth.

A low moan sounded in her throat. Her arms crept around his neck. Her fists curled in his hair and sent him spiraling over the edge. Something deep and feral snapped within him.

His teeth scraped her bottom lip. She whimpered and stiffened, straining against his embrace. He jerked away, buried his face in her neck and mumbled an apology.

Lorelei eased back, as though afraid if she moved too fast, one or both of them would break apart and crumble to the ground.

"What in the world just happened? I have never been moved by a single kiss the way you move me."

"Nor have I." He nuzzled his way to her ear then jaw.

"Yeah right. You're much too good a kisser to make me believe that."

A chuckle rumbled through him. Tentacles

of need crawled along every nerve in his body. "Believe me, sweet Lorelei, I've not kissed, nor been kissed, as thoroughly by another."

She untangled herself from his arms and stepped away. "Yeah, well I think we need to slow down. Things could get complicated, and we both need to keep a clear head."

He nodded then glanced at his watch. "You're right and I've got to get going. I'm late already."

Still, he hesitated. "Maybe I should call in a sub."

Lorelei shook her head. "No. You go. I won't get a single thing accomplished if you're underfoot all day."

He smirked. "OK. Promise you'll stay alert and keep Laurel under close scrutiny."

"I always am and do."

He grinned. "Promise, anyway."

Her laughter rang like chimes in the wind. His heart leapt in response. Another quick caress of his lips over hers and he left.

****

The days rolled quickly into weeks and the three of them slipped into a routine. Princess accompanied Lorelei during the day. At night she slept with Laurel, who seemed to rest better.

171

The episode which prompted Carson to purchase the animal occurred a time or two, though not as severe. Lorelei began to wonder if she'd been mistaken about the degree of Laurel's perceptiveness, or if having the dog made her daughter feel safer.

The weekends found them with Carson at one or the other's home.

A month after the storm, she and Carson sat on the front porch admiring their newly repaired vehicles while Laurel and Princess played in the front yard. Huge, puffy clouds drifted in a powder blue sky. She sighed. "Beautiful day."

He reached over and caressed her cheek with the back of his hand. "Not as lovely as the person sharing it with me."

Heat warmed her cheeks. She smiled at him. "Works both ways.

Giggles and a happy bark greeted her ears. Contentment rose in her breast. "Thank you for setting up and attending the meetings with the principal, sheriff, and guidance counselor. Seems now, we can't make a move about town without someone stopping to talk and pray with us."

He smiled. "You're welcome. That's what I like about this place."

"Me too. This is the most peace I believe I've

ever experienced in my life. I thank God every day for bringing us here.

He stroked her face again. "So do I."

Lorelei grabbed his hand and rested her cheek in his palm for a moment, then laced her fingers through his. "I'll be done with your back yard before long. Not sure what Mr. Flaven has for me next, but I've been thinking about starting my own landscaping service. I've designed business cards and brochures and I'm considering a website. What do you think—is there enough work around here?"

Carson shrugged. "I don't know about this town alone. However, with Nashville less than a half-hour away, and all the surrounding communities, I'd imagine you can build quite a business... but..." He hesitated.

Her eyebrow arched in question. "But what?"

"I wish you'd contemplate waiting a while before you venture too far out on your own, especially with Jaxon on the loose."

She bristled. "I refuse to hide any longer. If he finds us, I'll deal with him once and for all."

"I'm not asking you to hide, but to consider not advertising too far out. Business cards & brochures in neighboring towns could prove dangerous. And a website is like waving a red flag in front of an angry bull."

Frustration rose to choke her, but she knew he was right. *Oh God, will we ever be free?"*

His words haunted her in the weeks that followed. Halloween approached and with it, fears of the unknown. Though Lorelei felt safe and secure with the townsfolk, she hated the thought of all those costumes and what they could hide.

Carson arrived at Lorelei's house as planned on All Hallows Eve to find her and Laurel locked in a battle of wills.

"What's going on?"

Tears glistened on Laurel's cheeks. She brushed them away with an angry swipe.

"Mom won't let me trick-or-treat without you two accompanying me like I'm some kind of baby!"

"I said you could if you took Princess with you."

Laurel stomped her foot. "If I take her with me, everyone will know who I am!"

Lorelei took a step closer to her daughter, her hands clenched into fists by her side. "Another word, young lady and you won't go at all! The point of this night is to dress up and have fun. It doesn't matter if someone guesses who you are."

Carson stepped between them. "OK, let's calm down. I'm sure we can work something out."

Lorelei drew herself to her full five-feet-four. Her eyes flashed like emerald daggers. "Don't you dare get between me and my daughter. This is none of your business."

"Oh great, now everyone's fighting!" Laurel screeched before he could respond then stormed from the room.

Lorelei fumed. A low growl sounded in her throat. She raised her clenched fist and shook it under his nose. "Now look what you've done. Are you happy?"

Carson grabbed her hand, wrapped his other arm around her waist, and went nose-to-nose with her. "Don't shake your fist in my face, Lorelei Connor. I suggest you calm down and talk rationally."

"Or what?"

His senses heightened as every bit of her tension seeped into him. Her concerns popped into his mind, and he understood. He loosened his grasp and brushed his lips over her white knuckles. Releasing her hand, he cradled her cheek in his palm. "United we stand, divided we fall, Lore."

He urged her a notch closer and lowered his lips to hers. She stiffened a bit then melted against him. Within moments she was more than a passive participant in the kiss. Her arms curled around his neck; fingers wove through his hair. She whimpered and clung.

Passion raced through his veins like a heady drug. Visions of them, flesh to flesh and heart to heart, danced in his head. He pulled her closer still and devoured the lush nectar of her mouth.

A slamming door jerked him back to reality.

He broke the kiss, buried her face in his chest and held her tight, afraid if either of them tried to move, their trembling legs would give way. She quivered in his arms. Soft sobs escaped her and tore at his heart.

"I'm so afraid."

"I know. But there is nothing to worry about. I'm here. The whole town is here. Besides, I don't feel the least bit of apprehension."

She stepped back and looked into his eyes. Her gaze glowed like sunset atop a brilliant green forest. He saw clear to her soul, felt the anxiety flow out of her body.

Her eyebrow arched. Lips twitched. "So now I guess you think you can waltz in anytime and bend me to your will with a single kiss."

He laughed. "I wouldn't dare to be so presumptuous."

She smiled and his heart took flight. He brushed his lips over hers in a brief caress.

"What do you say we let Laurel walk with

her friends and then follow in the SUV? We'll keep Princess in the vehicle with the windows down so she can keep the kids in her sight and within her range of smell. At the slightest hint of unease, the first growl or whimper, we'll turn the dog loose."

"Sounds good to me."

"You think Laurel will agree?"

She snorted. "Laurel will agree, or she won't go."

He hummed and caressed her mouth with his. "Tough love is so sexy on you."

He moved away from her enticing embrace then called Laurel back into the room. Her tear-streaked face and stormy eyes tugged at his heart. "Laurel, your mom has agreed to allow you to walk with your friends..."

His words trailed off when she pumped her hand in the air and exclaimed "yes!"

He held up a hand to ward off any more outbursts. "However, we will follow with Princess in the SUV. You're to stay within our sight at all times. Is that understood?"

Her expression clouded. The triumphant smile turned into a frown. "But..."

Lorelei drew in an angry hiss. Carson shook his head and cautioned her with a firm look then turned back to the child. "Not up for discussion, Laurel. Either we follow or you don't go. The choice is yours."

An hour later they drove to the school for Laurel to meet her friends. Trick-or-treating began. The evening passed without incident.

As Thanksgiving approached, more than a hint of winter chilled the air. Carson felt the change in atmosphere as acutely as the evolution of seasons. Dreams and visions haunted his nights. He talked with Julie on more than one occasion and begged for insight into Jaxon's method of operation, his strengths, and weaknesses.

"Terrorization. If he can threaten or intimidate then he controls the person and/or situation. If he is close, he'll strike when least expected. You need to bring them here, Carson. Come home for the holiday."

"Figured I wouldn't be welcome. You know something I don't?"

"Oh, Cars, you know everyone is over the shock and grief. You're always welcome. This is your home. It's been five years."

The anguish in her voice pierced him like a splinter in the heart. Carson scrubbed a hand over his eyes and swallowed the lump in his throat. "No one has said that Jules, except you and the twins. No letters. An occasional phone call, but no real conversations. I do receive a card for birthdays and gifts at Christmas which is wonderful. It's nice to know I'm remembered..."

"Cars," she interrupted, her tone sullen.

"Don't say it, Jules. I know the accident was not my fault. I tried to warn Mom and Dad not to go on that trip. They knew of this... gift or curse, whatever you want to call it, but wouldn't listen! I should have stopped them or changed their minds somehow."

"Carson, you couldn't have changed their minds if you wanted. God's will is still His will. Look at the chain of events. Even if their car hadn't broken down and been crushed by that eighteen-wheeler, the plane they were scheduled to be on crashed with only a few survivors. Who's to say they would have lived through that? I don't think they would have." She paused, blew out a breath.

"It was simply their time to go. Stop blaming yourself for things you couldn't control. And stop rejecting your gift as a curse. God has a reason for blessing you with these premonitions, these prophesies...whatever they are. Stop fighting Him. Let Him show you what to do, and how to use them for His glory and your–everyone's–good. Think about it."

He raked a hand through his hair. "OK. I'll let you know as soon as possible what we decide."

The situation came to a tumultuous head the weekend before school was due to break. Laurel and Princess were traipsing through the wooded area which surrounded his house looking for pinecones and berries she could use to make Thanksgiving and Christmas decorations.

He and Lorelei were out on the back patio she'd built as part of the landscape design their landlord chose. He'd tried to convince her they should go with him to Mississippi. "Julie is the only one who knows about you and Jaxon and she's the one insisting I bring you home with me for the holiday. Besides, my family isn't that way."

Her eyes widened in disbelief. "Says he who has barely spoken to said family in five years, much less visited them."

His jaw hardened at the sarcasm in her tone. "That's not fair! My parents died. This is a whole lot different than you sleeping with my sister's husband, regardless of how it all came about."

Her palm connected with his cheek. He grabbed her wrist. "That was uncalled for, Lorelei."

"So was your comment."

A yelp from Princess and scream from Laurel rent the air before he could respond. They scrambled to where the sounds came from and met her as she ran out of the woods.

Lorelei enfolded her daughter against her breast. "What's the matter?"

"A man," she panted out.

Carson bolted for the woods, calling for Princess. The two returned winded, but empty handed. "Tell me everything, Laurel."

"I started to feel uneasy, you know, like someone was watching me. So, I headed back this way when Princess growled and tore off in another direction. I saw a man. At least I think it was a man. Whoever it was, is dressed in black, and had a ski mask over his or her face. But the person moved like a man."

She trembled and moved closer to her mother. "Do you think it's Daddy?"

Lorelei hugged her daughter closer and then gazed up at Carson. "I don't know, sweetheart, but how would you feel about going to Mississippi with Carson over the holiday to visit his family?"

The child brightened. "Really? Oh, boy, I'd love that!"

"It's settled then." Relief resonated in Carson's tone.

"Let's go inside and see what we can do about tickets."

****

They took a redeye flight from Nashville to arrive at Hattiesburg-Laurel Regional Airport in the pre-dawn hours. Laurel, thank God, slept well before time to leave, and managed to get to the airport and on the plane with minimal drama and very little grumbling. Lorelei, however, couldn't seem to stop the whirlwind of her thoughts.

Was that Jaxon in the woods? Had he found them? Would he figure out they'd left and follow them to Mississippi? Would Carson's family accept her, or even him, for that matter? How would they feel about Laurel? Would they really need to know who her father was? On and on the questions went, like a merry-go-round on an unending cycle.

Carson, who had one arm around her waist and his head on her shoulder, mumbled and nuzzled her neck. Shivers of delight shimmered down her spine and she rested her cheek against the thick mop of caramel-colored hair beneath her face. She awoke with a jolt when the flight attendant's voice came over the intercom.

"Ladies and gentlemen, we're preparing for descent into Hattiesburg-Laurel Regional Airport. Please place your seats in an upright position and prepare for landing."

Carson urged Lorelei and Laurel to remain

seated. "Let's wait until the plane clears a bit."

When the last person passed their seats, he rose and gathered their carry-on luggage. The dread and uncertainty in Lorelei's gaze cut like a knife in his heart but he had no idea how to reassure her. The three made their way off the plane and waited in baggage claim for Princess to be unloaded.

Animals could be heard whining, but his dog lay like a champ in her kennel without the slightest whimper. That is, until she spotted Laurel. He chuckled at her pitiful howls.

"Can I pet her a little bit?" Laurel asked.

He picked up the kennel. "Yeah, a little."

They walked to an unoccupied area, and he allowed Laurel to open the door of the cage long enough for a few quick pats and hugs.

"Why don't you go ahead to the rental car station, and we'll wait right here for you," Lorelei suggested.

Carson shook his head. "I'm not leaving you two alone with her locked up in this thing. Once she settles down, we'll go together."

An hour later they were loaded up and on their way. Carson glanced at his watch and realized though his family may be rising, it was still too early for them to bombard the house. He glanced in Lorelei's direction. "How about we make a pass through a drive-in for breakfast and find someplace Princess can run for a bit?"

"That would be great," Lorelei said.

"Yeah, I'm starved." Laurel chimed.

Carson grinned and winked at her in the rearview mirror. "You're always starved."

He pulled into the first fast-food place that served breakfast and placed their orders then drove to a roadside park with a designated pet area.

"Why don't you take Princess for a quick run, Laurel? Then we'll eat."

She did. Five minutes later she joined him and Lorelei at the picnic table. Once seated, she chattered away, asking questions about his family.

Lorelei rubbed her temples with a weary groan. "Laurel, please."

Carson laughed. "It's OK. I guarantee you'll meet every member of my family before the weekend is over."

Laurel finished her meal and then ran off with Princess again. Carson rose to throw away the trash then held a hand toward Lorelei. "Let's take a walk."

They strolled around the park, careful to keep Laurel and Princess in sight. When they returned, Carson rested against the picnic table and pulled her in his arms. He lifted her chin in a tender gesture and waited until she raised a wary gaze to meet his. "Do you trust me, Lorelei?"

She nodded.

"Good. Because we have nothing without trust. I guarantee everything will be fine, so try to relax and enjoy yourself. OK?"

She blinked hard to stop the flood of tears and swallowed hard.

He traced her bottom lip with his thumb. His voice softened. "I love you, Lorelei. I won't let anything happen to you or Laurel."

Lorelei wrapped her arms around his waist and rested her cheek against his heart. "I love you, too."

He held her until the morning chill seeped through the warmth of their jackets. Shifting her in his embrace, he brushed his lips over hers in a sweet caress then whistled for Laurel and Princess. Everyone loaded up and buckled in.

Carson drove the few miles to his home on the outskirts of town. He pulled into the drive and stopped in front of the old house. A poignant silence filled the vehicle. "Oh, man, I've missed this place."

Before anyone could utter a response, the door flew open, and people bounded down the steps. Carson bolted out of the truck to be swept into a group hug. Princess tugged against the hold Laurel had on her and woofed and whined, until Carson opened the truck door and let her out.

Laurel climbed out behind the dog, and he introduced her to his twin brothers and sister. Then he walked around to Lorelei's side of the vehicle.

Lorelei didn't wait for Carson to open her door. She did so herself and stepped out. Every ounce of trepidation vanished the moment she looked into his sister's eyes. The woman enfolded her in an embrace so strong Lorelei thought she might snap in two.

"I am so happy to meet you," Julie said, and moved back to lock gazes with her.

Lorelei smiled. "Same here."

Julie laughed—a rich infectious sound that had her smiling in return.

"No, you weren't. Admit it now, you were terrified."

Heat rose in her cheeks, but Lorelei's gaze didn't waver. She nodded. "I *was* terrified. But not anymore."

Julie draped her arm around Lorelei's waist. "Good. Let's go inside and visit while Carson unloads the truck." She turned to her brother. "I'll put a fresh pot of coffee on for when you're done. Then you all look as though you could use a nap."

Carson and the twins grabbed suitcases, and

everyone went into the house cackling and talking all at once. The next few days were both celebration and reunion. His entire family gathered to welcome him home and embraced Lorelei and Laurel as though they were long-lost friends. The three of them flew out again early Sunday afternoon to get ready for school and work the next day.

****

As they usually do, the weeks between Thanksgiving and Christmas flew by in a flurry of activity. The closer Christmas drew near, the more restless the kids became. Holiday programs, festivities, and shopping filled every spare moment of time, until Carson couldn't breathe.

Though the trip home at Thanksgiving had been a welcome reprieve, visions, dreams, and premonitions returned with fervor and intensity. He prayed and sought God early and often. Careful not to instill fear in them, he admonished Lorelei and Laurel to remain alert to their surroundings. They would drive to Mississippi this time and he looked forward to the two-week break.

Two hours into the trip they stopped at a convenience store for snacks and a potty break.

Carson stood at the counter in line with his purchases when Lorelei walked up beside him, her hands equally full of drinks and junk food. "Where's Laurel?"

"She went to the restroom."

The restroom was outside and around the back of the building. Goosebumps rose on his arms. The hair on the back of his neck stood up. "Alone?"

The tone of his voice must have alerted her. Both dropped their items on the counter and rushed out. Princess was tearing up the truck in an effort to get out. Carson pulled the door open. The dog shot out and ran around the building, barking like a rabid animal. They followed but were brought up short by the sight that greeted them.

Laurel struggled against Jaxon as he tried to drag her through the wooded area behind the store. "Mom!"

Jaxon turned to face them and held a gun to Laurel's head. "Come near and I'll shoot her."

Carson and Lorelei skidded to a stop. Princess lunged and grabbed Jaxon by the arm. He shook her off, and, with one shot, felled her attempt to rescue Laurel.

"No!" Laurel screamed. "You killed my dog!"

Jaxon turned her in his arms and tried to

console the distraught child. "I had to, honey. Don't you see, she wants to keep you from me, too? You're my child. I only want to have you in my life." His whiny tone took on an angry edge. "Your mother has forced me to stay away from you."

He turned, pointed the gun at Lorelei. "You! You've stolen my child. I ought to kill you right now while I have the chance."

"No!" Laurel's voice cut through the air. "I'll go with you, Daddy. We'll be together."

"Jaxon, please, we can work something out." Lorelei said, but he shook his head.

"You lie."

"No. Honestly."

The sound of sirens rent the air. A panicked look clouded Jaxon's face. "You, get over here." He pointed the gun at Lorelei when she hesitated. "Now!"

Carson grabbed her arm. "Lorelei, no."

She shook him off and ran to meet them. Jaxon aimed the gun at Carson. "If you try to stop us, I'll kill you and then I'll kill them." He hesitated, confusion evident in his demeanor. "Don't I know you?"

"Remain silent."

The dictated words were clear in Carson's mind. He shook his head.

The sirens drew closer. Jaxon grabbed

Laurel's hand and shoved Lorelei forward. "Keep moving."

Carson gave them a head start then followed at a safe distance. He ducked behind a tree and watched Jaxon push Laurel and Lorelei into the backseat of a car. Dashing to where he could see the license plate, he committed the identifying numbers to mind. Jackson lunged into the driver's seat and sped away, throwing dust and gravel in his wake.

Carson ran back through the woods and rushed to the counter. "He kidnapped them and shot my dog! Where does the road directly behind here and through the woods go? In which direction does it run?"

The cashier's eyes widened with fright. "I... I'm not from here."

Carson spit out a curse and turned to the people in line. "Does anyone know?"

"The road runs north and south." Someone answered, waving his hand. "Which way did they head?"

Carson pointed.

"That's north. If you turn right out of the parking lot and keep going, the two roads will intersect about three miles out."

"Thanks!" He hurried to his vehicle and tore out of the parking lot. Calm washed over him. Direction followed. As though in a trance, he pressed the button on the hands-free cell phone device clipped on his sun visor and, using the voice-activated feature, called the police.

As concise as possible he relayed information as to where they were, what road they were on and which direction they headed. He gave the plate number of the car Jaxon drove and listened while the dispatcher barked commands over the radio. When addressed again, he told of Princess and asked them to send a veterinarian over to pick her up.

His brain remained lucid while his spirit groaned in supplication. *God, please! Watch over them. Shield them under your mighty wings. Send forth Your angels to guard and protect.*

"Where are you now? Do you see the suspect?"

"I'm think that's them straight ahead." He sped up, noted the plate number. "Yes, it's them."

"OK. Back off," the officer ordered. "He doesn't know what you're driving does he?"

"Not that I'm aware of."

"Good. Be careful not to get too close. Don't crowd him. Just stay with him and keep us informed. I've got officers on the way and roadblocks being set up ahead."

Carson let up on the accelerator and allowed

a car to pass, getting between him and Jaxon, but kept the vehicle in his sight. His mind circled around the officer's questions.

Did Jaxon know what he drove? How did he find them? At what point did he recognize them and follow? How come he didn't sense anything amiss until Laurel went to the restroom alone? Why didn't God warn him?

The road curved to the right and for a moment he lost sight of them. He breathed a sigh of relief when the car between them turned off. He sped up a notch and moved in a bit closer. His heart clenched when Jaxon pointed the gun over the seat and waved it at them. Lorelei shielded Laurel with her body, and glanced out the back window, terror etched in every plane of her face.

Her eyes widened, expression changed, and Carson knew she realized he was behind them. He placed a finger to his lips to indicate she should remain calm and silent. He gave her thumbs up and twirled a finger to indicate she should turn around, glad when she complied.

Panic gripped his soul when Jaxon swerved into an abandoned field so suddenly that his car started to fishtail and spun out of control. The scene unfolded before him in slow motion as the car flipped and rolled.

"Oh, God, no!"

Horror escalated into anger. "I'll never forgive You for this! I'll never speak to You again if they die!"

A frantic voice over the cell phone caught his attention. "What happened? Where are you?"

Carson screeched his truck to a halt within feet of Jaxon's car and relayed the information. "He lost control. Rolled the car."

He could see it all and talked fast, even as he unclipped his seatbelt and opened the door. "The driver was slung out of the car but is pinned beneath it. He's not moving. I don't know about the passengers."

"Don't get out of your vehicle."

"I can't just leave them there!"

"I need you to stay calm. And stay in your vehicle. Where are you?"

His heart hammered in his throat as Carson looked around and gave landmarks.

"OK, we're in route. Hang tight."

Within seconds, emergency vehicles swarmed the area. Police approached with caution. Guns drawn. When one shook his head and holstered his firearm, Carson exited his vehicle. His legs nearly collapsed.

He leaned on the hood and forced air in and out of his lungs as paramedics rushed in to extricate Lorelei and Laurel from the back seat. He nearly fainted when both crawled out, refusing the stretchers nearby. He stepped closer. Lorelei turned, met his gaze, and flew into his arms. Laurel followed on her mother's heels.

Carson enfolded them in his embrace, sobbing with relief. "Oh, thank God. Thank You, God."

"Sir, Ma'am?" A hesitant voice cut through the joy. "We really need to check you ladies out. Please, get in the ambulance and let's go to the hospital. I know you both feel fine, but we need to be sure."

Carson stepped back but held them an arms-length away. "He's right. You two get in the ambulance. I'll be right behind you."

"The police will need statements too," the paramedic said.

"I'll follow you to the hospital," an officer announced. "The others can clean up here."

Laurel hesitated, her eyes darting to the scene as firemen up righted the car. "Daddy?"

Lorelei pulled her close as the officer shook his head. "He's dead, honey. I'm sorry."

Laurel began to cry. "Why does it hurt so much? He deserved to die! He was so mean, and he killed Princess. It shouldn't hurt so much."

Carson wrapped his arms around Laurel and Lorelei once more. "No one deserves to die like this, honey. Regardless of anything he did, he was still your father. Come on now; let's get you and mom to the hospital. We can sort this all out later."

He waited until both were loaded safely into the ambulance then hurried to his truck to follow. A police unit brought up the rear as the three vehicles sped off to the nearest hospital.

Carson paced outside the ER waiting area while he put a call through to Julie and explained why they would be late.

"Are they all right? What about Jaxon?" Her voice, frantic with worry, cut over the line.

Carson relayed the accident play-by-play. "It's a miracle they're alive, much less unhurt."

"Yeah, but it's a shame about Princess."

He wiped the moisture off his cheeks. "I'll see if the veterinarian will keep her until after the holidays. We'll pick her up on our way home and bury her in the yard."

"Good idea. I'll let you go now. Call me when Laurel and Lorelei are released, and you're on your way here."

Four hours later the girls were released with what the doctors claimed to be a miraculous event. Both were given pain medication for the bumps and bruises. Satisfied with their statements, the police assured they would contact them should the need arise for more information.

Jaxon's family would be called to retrieve his body, but both Carson and Lorelei offered to handle burial expenses should no relatives be found to take care of him.

Carson asked for directions and drove to the veterinary clinic where Princess was taken. Pained silence filled the lobby while they waited to speak to the veterinarian. An elderly gentleman walked out and shook hands with Carson and Lorelei. With a twinkle in his eye, he put an arm around Laurel.

"I'll take you to see her, but you have to stay calm."

Laurel blinked back tears and nodded.

He led the way with Laurel. Carson and Lorelei followed. When they neared a tiny room, he turned with a grin and wink, then opened the door with a flourish.

Princess raised her head and whined. Her tail thumped wildly. Laurel rushed over to the bed and put her arms around the dog's neck. "You're alive!"

"Be gentle, young lady." The vet explained that the bullet went straight through the dog without hitting any vital organs. He'd picked her up, then cleaned and stitched her wounds. "A few weeks of rest and pampering, and she will be good as new. I'd like to keep her overnight though. For observation."

"Sure." Carson and Lorelei said in unison.

Laurel lifted wide, pleading eyes to the veterinarian. "Can I stay, too?"

Guffaws filled the air. The man shook his head. "I don't have anywhere for you to sleep, sweetheart. There's a bed and breakfast two blocks down the road. I'll call if there is any change in her condition—which there won't be. I've done this long enough to guarantee she'll be right as rain, and ready to travel, within a day or two."

Lorelei put her arm around her daughter and gave her a hug. "Let's go get settled in at the B&B. We'll come back later to check on her."

Laurel hesitated and eyed the vet. "You promise?"

He chortled. "Of course. I'll be here all night with her, so you can come by or call any time."

With a reluctant frown, she hugged the dog once more then followed her mother and Carson to the truck.

The next morning Carson met with the detectives investigating the incident while Lorelei and Laurel stayed with Princess at the veterinarian's office.

"I have a couple of questions for you."

The officer leaned back in his chair and clasped his hands behind his head. "Ask away."

"Do you have any idea how this guy found

us? We live in a very small town and neither of us has ever seen him nor his vehicle. And believe me, we, as well as the whole town, have been on the lookout for him for months."

"Honestly, I think it was plain circumstance he spotted you all. Turns out he's lived in this town for a few weeks. We've had a rash of burglaries in the surrounding communities but couldn't pin down the culprit. We uncovered enough evidence in the vehicle and in his apartment to convict and send him to prison for a very long time had he lived through this."

Carson breathed a sigh of relief that he hadn't missed God in the chaos of the preceding weeks. He thanked the officer and left. Three days later, the trio and their canine companion made the remainder of the six-hour trip from Stars Crossing, Tennessee to Laurel, Mississippi.

Christmas Eve, Carson, and Lorelei took a walk under a moonless sky. One star, high in the heavens, shone bright upon the earth. Peace filled the air.

Carson pulled Lorelei in his arms and raised her gloved fingers to his lips. Dissatisfied with the taste of leather, he cupped her face in his hands and lowered his mouth to hers. What he intended to be a sweet, tender gesture, turned all-too-quickly into a heated embrace. He ended the kiss in slow, measured degrees, until she lay limp against his chest.

He swallowed the heart clogging his airways and cleared his throat. "I asked you once and you refused to marry me due to the circumstances. Will you marry me, now?"

In answer, Lorelei smiled up at him and rose on tiptoe, her lips reaching up to receive his once more.

The End

Dear Reader,

For those of you who've been with me through the long-haul, I THANK YOU for your continued love and support.

For my new readers, I hope you're not disappointed.

Life and circumstance have a way of beating us down until we feel totally lost and alone, or so low you have to reach up to touch bottom. For those covered in Christ this is not so! No matter how difficult your situation may be, please remember you are always in HIS sight and never too far down in the pit that HE can't reach down and pull you out.

If you don't know Him already, I pray that you too, will pursue a relationship with the Lord

Jesus. If you do know Him, call upon Him in your time of trouble, for He will hear and answer.

As always, may God bless and keep you—and yours—in the palm of His mighty hand.

Journey's End

Ellie Thibaudeau walked around her property for the seventh time in prayer, placing a hedge of protection around her home and business. As she did each year at the onslaught of hurricane season. A combination bookstore, souvenir shop, and antique/vintage flea market, *Thib's Treasures* had been handed down for generations. From her grandparents to her parents and now to her. One day, soon, it would go to her daughter's daughter.

If she wanted it.

Ellie had been a wanderer her entire life. A free spirit who'd never settled in one place longer than a few years. Until Sheila came along. The only good thing that came out of her brief, disastrous relationship with a narcissistic musician hellbent on self-destruction.

Needing help and support to raise her daughter after her partner's death, Ellie returned to her hometown of Wellington, Florida. Unfortunately, Sheila took after her father more than mother and had followed in his footsteps. But not before leaving another child for Ellie to raise.

Callyn Shayne Thibaudeau, Ellie's Angel Girl, resembled her grandmother in so many ways. The thick, reddish-brown hair—though

Ellie's sported more gray now. Merry hazel eyes which turned green or brown depending on their mood or the clothes they wore. Fair-to-olive complexion that burned easily but once started, tanned beautifully. A zest for life, love, and laughter.

Itchy feet.

Which is why Callyn jetted off to Greece last weekend. She intended to shop for antiques while there, but Ellie knew her granddaughter's MFA degree and PACC certification were nothing but excuses to travel far and wide.

She'd have done the same had she not fallen head over heels for the man who'd sired Callyn's mother.

Enough reminiscing. Ellie shook herself mentally and opened the shop's windows and shutters to let the sea breeze in. She turned the sign on the door to 'Open' and walked back through the store. Lighting candles. Rearranging items on shelves. Tweaking displays. Swiping at dust that danced on sunbeams in the air.

The bell on the door announced the arrival of a customer. Ellie turned with her smile in place and froze as the most gorgeous male she'd ever seen strode through the entryway. Her heart stuttered then took off at a gallop. Tiny bubbles of blood burst beneath her skin. Her breath caught in an audible hiss. She swallowed the hard knot of shyness in her throat. "M-may I help you?"

Her voice made him think of windchimes and fairies. Sean Boyle shoved a lock of silver hair out of his eyes and grinned. "Aye. Ye can tell me how to get to MacGregor's Pub on the strand and join me fer a drink there later."

A melodious vibration bubbled up from her throat and set his heart to racing. Sean couldn't get past the sound long enough to understand the words that followed. Her query as to whether he was all right and touch, like fire and silk on his arm, nearly sent him into a swoon. "Would ye mind saying that again, sweetheart?"

"I'll do better than that." She grabbed a piece of paper and pen from the counter and drew him a map with written directions to the pub.

He covered her hand with his, raised it to his lips. "Thank you. Ye will meet me for a drink later, won't ye?"

"I don't close shop until five. Surely, you're not going to stay at the pub that late."

"I'll stay all night if I have to."

Her smile took his breath away. "I won't leave here unless I have yer word."

She giggled.

His stomach clenched like a nervous fist

until she agreed to meet him at five-thirty.

Sean left the small trinket shop and headed to MacGregor's pub. One of his oldest mates had badgered him for years to visit. Especially after his wife passed. He, like many Irishmen married late in life and honored his vows unto death. Now, with his children grown, Sean decided the time to visit his friend had come.

He had no idea he'd meet the woman of his dreams on his first day in America. Oh, he'd loved his wife. But theirs was a quiet kind of affection based on mutual caring and respect.

Nothing like the soul thrilling excitement he experienced at the resonance of the shopkeeper's voice.

Sean realized he'd never even asked her name! He slapped a palm to his forehead and cursed himself for every kind of fool.

Maybe Colin would know.

Turns out Colin knew a lot about the proprietor of *Thib's Treasures* and had no problem sharing that information with Sean over a couple of Guinnesses and huge servings of Shepherd's pie. That afternoon she walked into the pub, and his heart missed a beat. Sean met her at the door and led her to a table where they talked for hours. As though they'd known each other forever.

Or maybe in another life.

The idea that they shared one or more past lives was no stretch of the imagination for a man who believed in fairies and leprechauns.

As the night eased into morning, Sean took her hands in his and gazed into her beautiful eyes. "All me life I've searched for a woman whose mere presence filled me with joy. Looks like my journey's ended."

Ellie smiled. "Looks like mine is just beginning."

The End

Dear Reader,

We've all had instances where we *felt* something or "known" someone at first meeting. This is normal and a natural extension of Who we are. Not the ego-based personality we show to the world, but at our core. We are spiritual beings having a human experience. We pick up "vibes" on an energetic level.

This is our intuition—an innate ability that connects us all and guides us through impulses of the heart. Let us not be too quick to discount these instances but be curious and seek to find the truth about ourselves, our God, our Angels, Guides, and each other.

Something to think about!

Review of Love

Judge not, that you be not judged. For with what judgment you judge, you will be judged also. (Matthew 7:1-2)

Jason Stockwell watched from his small patio as Kylie rounded the corner and then jogged up the stairs to her apartment. As was his custom, he fantasized about following in her wake and... His breath jagged in and out of his lungs, heart thundered in his chest, palms sweated. The sound of running water upstairs didn't help his state of mind as he envisioned her in the shower.

He closed his eyes and willed his emotions into some semblance of order. He raised the coffee cup to his mouth. His hand shook. The scorching liquid burned his tongue. A curse hissed between his lips. *Not again! Should have known it was still too hot.*

To say Kylie Erickson intrigued him would be the understatement of the century. His infatuation had begun five years ago, in college. They'd taken several writing and journalism classes together, but he'd never had the intestinal fortitude to ask her for a date. He always knew she was destined for greatness, and he'd followed her career, silently cheering her on with each accomplishment. Then, a year ago ***The Sparkling Star Report*** commissioned him to review her work and interview her.

He'd already purchased and read every book she'd written. Therefore, the assignment was both pleasure and agony. Rereading and reviewing each novel was pure joy, and the evaluations appeared in an on-going segment in the popular magazine. Though the publication was known as a "rag mag," he did his best to present an honest and straightforward opinion of each book and every interview he produced.

Unable to secure an appointment with the prolific author, he was thrilled when she moved into his apartment building in the unit above the one in which he lived. He'd hatched a plan to coax her into an interview, but he could barely bring himself to approach her.

Hence his agony.

He couldn't get over his innate shyness to share more than a few words, much less have a meaningful conversation, with her. It hadn't taken her long to recognize him as the SSR reporter, and from that day, ignore him.

The fact her erratic schedule drove him insane didn't help. Up all hours of the night, the movement in her apartment kept him awake more than he slept. But like clockwork, every morning at seven, she bounded down the steps for a run.

Realizing the sound of running water had been replaced by absolute silence, he glanced up and wondered with star-struck, romantic imaginings what she might be doing now.

God, help me.

More desperate plea than rational prayer, he couldn't help but smile when the newspaper landed at his feet with a thud and brought him back to reality.

"Jesus, I don't know what it's going to take for this woman to agree to an interview, nor can I seem to get her out of my mind long enough to finish that last review. I'm running out of time here, and I'd sure appreciate it if You open a door."

A chuckle echoed in his mind. Mocked. Jason wondered if God was laughing at the predicament, he'd gotten himself into, or if the sound stemmed from the devil ridiculing his faith. He picked up the newspaper and his now-cold coffee and trod indoors to see if he could take up where he left off in her latest novel.

Perhaps a raving review would lure her out of her shell, *or cave*, and she'd grace him with a few words that he could polish to create an interview.

Or, maybe once he finished the review, he could actually ask her opinion of it before he sent it to his editor. Then, if she saw that he really did do quality work, that he admired her and didn't want to do her harm, she might give him that interview.

Hope beat a tattoo in his heart as he poured a fresh cup of coffee and placed his laptop on the table.

****

Kylie twisted her hair into a thick braid. Refreshed from her run and subsequent shower, she prepared a light breakfast and took it onto the balcony which overlooked a huge meadow flocked with wildflowers. Bees and butterflies danced among the Columbine, Milkweed and Larkspur.

She nibbled on her toast and let the peaceful scene soak into her spirit while her mind roamed idly along the trajectory of her career until it circled back to her current work in progress. She considered and discarded solutions to the corner her characters had written themselves into.

What am I overlooking? I know there are holes in the subplot but can't begin to see where they are.

The wailing cry of a cat followed by the opening and closing of a door, jerked her back into the present moment and thrust her into the quagmire that had hindered the flow of words onto the page for weeks.

Her usually placid temper jumped into a simmer.

It's all Jason Stockwell's fault!

She'd recognized the shy, geeky guy from college when he emailed her after her first novel hit the charts. During college, she'd thought he was cute, so she didn't mind sharing occasional correspondence over the years. In fact, she was flattered that he was one of her biggest fans and had wondered why he never asked her out.

His initial request for an interview came as a pleasant surprise. Until she found out what publication he wrote for. She did not want to be associated with a gossip rag.

She'd avoided him since then. Discovering she'd inadvertently moved into his apartment building she'd almost forfeited the first and last month's rent, along with the deposit money she'd forked out, and found another place to live. Had the place not been such a great location, she might've been able to swallow losing the small fortune.

Maybe not. Her career was on the upswing but throwing money down the drain simply to avoid a reporter—college mate or not—was silly.

Raking her chair back from the table, she

rose, picked up her plate and went into her apartment. She rinsed her dishes and wandered into the living room.

Something's gotta change.

On a surge of inspiration, she mixed some cleaning solution in a bucket of water and decided to clean and rearrange her entire living area. All 1200 feet of it. Hopefully the physical cleansing would somehow erase the cobwebs from her creativity.

****

Jason's optimism vanished. Peace and quiet—and the flow of thoughts and words— ended with a thud from the upstairs apartment. Followed by the thump and bump of music so loud he swore a herd of elephants did the rumba. The occasional scrape and grind of furniture across the floor interrupted the dance.

Trying to concentrate, he turned on a white noise app, switched to earbuds and eventually resorted to ear plugs. All to no avail. An hour later, he flung back from the table with such force the chair toppled. Quick thinking and narrow vision enabled him to see, and catch, his laptop as it slid toward the floor.

A low growl sounded in his throat as he stormed out of his apartment and up the stairs.

Past the point of a civil knock, he banged on her door. She opened it with a flourish. He stormed through without waiting for an invitation.

"Excuse me, Mr. Stockwell, but you're not welcome here!"

"Well, excuse me, *Ms. Erickson*, but you're the most inconsiderate, stubborn, self-centered woman I've ever met. How do you expect me to get any work done with the racket going on up here?"

She whirled away with a snort and turned down the music. "I wouldn't deign to call what you do work. But there, are you happy?"

"I'll be happy when you treat me like a person and be as respectful of my time and work as I am of yours."

"Person? More like passive-aggressive stalker. Half the time you act like you can't wait for that interview. The other half, you behave as though it would take an act of God for you to even speak to me."

"Passive-aggressive stalker? You want assertive-aggressive, instead? I'll show you, lady." He pulled her into his arms. His lips swooped over hers in a scorching kiss. Within moments everything about the embrace softened. When the kiss ended with her plastered against him, her fists curled into his hair.

After a few moments of stunned silence, she pushed herself out of his arms. Her palm connected with his cheek in a resounding slap. Jason stepped back and used every ounce of self-control he possessed to refrain from touching her again. He turned and strode from her apartment and down the stairs into his own. He plopped in his chair and started to write.

Peppered with adjectives like selfish, stuck-up, and eccentric, words poured forth with scathing clarity. Within moments he had not only a raving review, but an interview as well. He'd get her with this for sure!

His editor would absolutely love it.

His finger trembled over the 'send' button.

****

Kylie paced, careful to be quiet. Three days had passed since her neighbor stormed into her apartment, swept her well-ordered life into turmoil, and left her schedule in shreds. She never believed in writer's block or anything like it.

Nevertheless, the nasty cloud of stymied imagination hung over her head. Every time she sat at the computer, her mind froze, fingers locked up tighter than a... She shook her head and flushed at the analogy that came to mind.

Even her thoughts were not her own!

She closed her eyes to pray but all she saw, all she felt, was his blistering gaze and searing lips.

Why had she not stopped him? Why hadn't she called the cops? The guy had practically forced himself on her!

OK, maybe not. She had kind of provoked him with her insults, and even though he'd grabbed her, she never actually felt… *accosted*… but… but still, that didn't give him the right to—

No one had ever devastated her with a single kiss before! For the life of her, Kylie couldn't get past it. He'd touched some place deep inside. A part she'd never allowed anyone to reach before.

The cute, shy guy from college, the one who could barely say two words to her, had scaled the walls of her heart in a way she would not have normally let pass. What was wrong with her?

A sob shivered through her. *Why God? Why him?*

Why not?

The words echoed in the depths of her soul.

Because he's a… A parasite! He writes for a rag mag for goodness sakes. I want a man who respects me. Respects my craft. Not someone who uses his ability to write gossip and ruin people's lives.

In other words, if a writer isn't a *big commercial success* he isn't really an author, right? Who made you the judge of talent, a gift I give out?

She felt the chastisement from the depths of her being. A flush climbed in her cheeks. Her heart trembled with shame.

Oh, Lord, I never thought of myself as that, but I guess that's what my actions have shown all along. I'm sorry.

Kylie knew God wasn't the only one she should apologize to. Without hesitation she marched downstairs and met Jason on his way up.

"I..." They began at the same time. A dark flush crept up his neck. Jason ran a hand through his hair and insisted she speak first.

"I wanted to apologize for not being considerate of your work schedule. Just because I can't seem to write a single word doesn't mean I should make everyone around me miserable too."

He smiled and her heart skipped a thud.

"I was on my way to apologize also. Barging in and kissing you that way is no way for a gentleman to behave toward a lady. I should've treated you with more respect. I can assure you I'm not usually that neanderthal. In fact, I've never actually done anything like that before."

As shy as he'd always been before, she believed him. The fact he still considered her a lady only succeeded in making her more ashamed of her judgmental attitude. She knew what she had to do.

Warmth flooded her cheeks. She gazed at him for a full moment. "Thank you. If you're still interested, I'll agree to the interview."

His entire face lit up when he smiled. "I'd really appreciate that. I've already got an outline, perhaps we can discuss it over dinner? Tomorrow night, six o'clock?"

Kylie swallowed the hard knot of nerves clogging her airways and nodded.

"Great! I'll see you tomorrow then. And Kylie? Thank you, too. You won't be sorry. I promise."

I hope not, she thought as he turned around and headed back down the stairwell.

The next evening, she stood at his door, heart pounding, hands shaking. She pushed the doorbell and heard a harried response. When he opened the door, her thundering heart punched its way into her throat then lunged to the pit of her stomach.

The towel tied loosely around his waist confirmed she'd interrupted his shower. His damp hair lay plastered against a perfectly shaped head. The dark mass, also moist, which curled up his chest, had her fingers hankering to reach out and stroke. Gold flecks danced in crystal green eyes. "Oh... uh... am I early?"

"I'm sorry, I'm running a bit behind."

Kylie opened her mouth to speak but no more words came. She stuttered, flushed then forced the lump of emotions down her dry throat, and tried again. "I'll go back up."

Jason hesitated a moment then opened the door in invitation and waved toward the small kitchen table. "Nonsense. Have a seat. I'll be right out."

She followed as gracefully as possible on legs that felt about as solid as wet pasta. Questions rolled around in her head. *What on earth am I doing? What kind of questions is he going to ask? I'm so nervous I doubt I can stomach the slightest morsel. Maybe we shouldn't go out, what kind of signal will dinner give him? God, help me.*

Shivers shook her entire being as she sat, but all she knew was she had to be obedient to the still, small voice inside whispering encouragement.

A meow snagged her attention. She bent to pet the fluffy calico rubbing against her legs. Her gaze landed on a wadded-up piece of paper beneath the table. She picked it up, smoothed it out as much as possible, and read. The blood drained from her face and gelled somewhere in the region of her feet at the sarcastic words contained within the review.

When Jason strolled into the kitchen, she couldn't bear to look at him, but when she finally raised her gaze to his, her eyes swam with tears. She blinked hard to stop the floodgate from bursting, stood, and held the paper toward him, hating the way her hand trembled. "Looks like I'm too late, you've already ruined me with this."

"Kylie, wait."

She shook her head to ward off his words. On a sudden burst of emotion, she crumbled the paper and threw it at him. "I hope you enjoy your revenge. And that you choke on it. I can't believe I fell for your sob-story apology!"

She turned on her heel wanting to get out of there before she had a complete melt down.

"No. Wait." He caught her by the arm, stopping her retreat.

She twirled around to face him. His hand slid down to grip her wrist loosely. Though technically, he'd grabbed her again, she could tell he strove to be gentle. His other hand skimmed up her side to caress her face.

"Sweet Kylie, that's not the review I intend to publish. That's the one I threw into the trash. Nosey has a habit of digging out balls of paper to play with. Would you like to see the finished, well, almost finished version?"

Warmth from those green eyes seeped into her heart, stole the angst from her mind. *Judge not lest ye be judged.* The scripture floated through her soul. She nodded.

He brushed his lips across her forehead, released her, and moved away to pick up a legal pad off the table beside his computer. She skimmed the review unable to tear her eyes away from the page. Flowery adjectives replaced every scornful word she'd read on the crumpled-up paper. The sweetness of his glowing prose rendered her ineffective in stemming the tears this time when Jason cupped her face in his hands and lowered his lips to hers in a tender embrace.

****

One year later headlines read: Celebrity Wedding Announcement!

Sources reveal former contributor to **The Sparkling Star Report,** Jason Stockwell, and best-selling author Kylie Erickson, exchanged vows in an intimate and very private ceremony on a moonlit beach beneath a blanket of stars. The couple is reportedly honeymooning in Star City, Ireland.

The End

Dear Reader,

As Christians we are instructed not to judge our fellow man. But like Kylie, many of us still do. My prayer is, like Kylie, we put aside our judgments and open our heart and mind to the people God puts in our lives.

If you don't know Him already, I pray you seek Jesus as your Lord and Savior. If you do, I urge you to pursue a closer, more personal walk with Him.

As always, THANK YOU for your continued support of my writing – may you find joy in reading.

Soul Mates

Jolie LeBlanc walked throughout the tiny log home opening windows to let in the fresh morning air. The scent of roux from the gumbo she made last night hung as thick inside as the smell of Magnolia did outside. Carrying a steaming cup of coffee, she stepped out onto the porch that wrapped three-quarters around her house and eased into the rocking chair. The silence of the predawn hours–her favorite time of day–filled her heart with gratitude and soul with peace.

Years of studying and researching abroad, her Masters in Archeology and Minor in Anthropology finally landed her here. Secluded on five acres of land on the English Bayou. In a house built over a century ago and supposedly haunted by the famed pirate, Jean Lafitte.

Having dealt with ancient cultures and folklore, the idea of ghosts didn't faze Jolie. Her studies in Paranormal Science paid off when she proved or disproved a "haunting."

She'd visited numerous places around the world that were rumored to be inhabited by spirits, but Jolie loved it when her ghost hunting could be combined with archeological digs. Sorting through ruins, gathering artefacts, and building, or bridging, the History around the people and cultures of the past always fascinated her.

Especially those she'd resided in, in millenniums past. Another lifetime. Another trip to Earth only to return to Heaven and come back again.

And again.

Looking for that forever love.

A shiver broke into her soul.

About time the contract they made in the afterlife, before life actually, was honored.

Oh, they'd connected numerous times throughout the millennia but their 'happy ever after' was usually cut short by 'till death do us part.'

Goosebumps rose on her skin. Her breath caught. Jolie leaned forward and listened. The dip and splash of a paddle slicing through the quiet gurgle of the bayou followed by the whisper of a pirogue or small flat-bottom boat, announced someone's approach.

Stepping off the porch, she walked toward the shore. A Blue Heron rose gracefully from where he had been fishing. A cacophony of insects joined the symphony of bird song. Jolie heard the splash of a frog or turtle as it returned to the water. She watched a raccoon waddle down to the edge of the bayou, fish out a large minnow and wash it, before sitting on its hind legs to enjoy the snack. An alligator glided slowly along the bank, undisturbed by the advancing canoe.

Jolie observed the shimmering image of a man as he disembarked the watercraft. Her heart raced when he turned and materialized fully. Every cell in her body recognized him...The dark brooding eyes, strong jaw, square chin, tiny scar slashed across his temple.

Their gazes touched.

Hearts connected.

Souls entwined.

"I've come. As promised."

Jolie slid into his arms and rested her head against his chest.

"At last," she breathed, lifting her lips to his for a long-awaited kiss.

The End

Dear Reader,

I've been fascinated with the supernatural for ages. I believe in miracles and magic. Not the dark or evil kind, but the mystical side of life where the idea of reincarnation or past lives are possibilities to be explored. Especially where romance is concerned. After all, how do we *know* when we've met our soul mate? Or found the perfect job? Or met the right person to help with our business venture?

I believe events like these are not coincidences, but God ordained synchronicities or activities of the soul. They're not something to fear but to consider, study, and investigate with the openness, wonderment, and innocence of a child.

Something to think about...

About the Author

Pamela S. Thibodeaux grew up in the town of Iowa, Louisiana. She is the mother of four (two by blood and two by marriage) and a grandmother. A deeply committed Christian, Pamela firmly believes in God and His promises.

"God is very real to me, and I feel people today need and want to hear more of His truths wherever they can glean them. People are hungry for practical (and real) Christian values, not some 'holier-than-thou' dictates which are impossible to believe and difficult to live up to," Pamela says.

"I do my best to encourage readers to develop a personal relationship with God. The deepest desire of my heart is to glorify God and to get His message of faith, trust, and forgiveness to a hurting world."

Email Pamela at:
pam@pamelathibodeaux.com
Visit her website:
http://www.pamelathibodeaux.com
Sign up to receive ***Pam's Newsletter*** and get a FREE short story.

Also: be sure to follow Pam on Social Media: FaceBook, Twitter @psthib, Instagram, Pinterest, GoodReads, and BookBub.

Other Titles by
Pamela S. Thibodeaux

<u>Tempered Hearts</u> (book 1 in Tempered series)

An innocent veterinarian. A jaded cowboy. Will they get burned under a Texas sun or find the heat that leads to happily ever after?

Craig Harris has sworn off relationships. He's been burned and betrayed too many times to count. But when he crosses paths with the hot-tempered veterinarian his grandfather hired for the summer will he let go of hurt and mistrust to find the true love he's always longed for?

Tamera Collins is in no mood to put up with an arrogant jerk cowboy even if he is her boss. Grieving too-recent losses leaves her wary of the strong attraction between her and Craig. Can she overcome heartache and shattered faith and open up to their blossoming love?

<u>Tempered Dreams</u> (book 2 in Tempered Series)

He took an oath to preserve life. Can he stick to it when the woman he loves is in jeopardy?

Dr. Scott Hensley (introduced in Tempered

Hearts) has built a wall around his heart since the death of his wife and parents. Katrina Simmons is recovering from scars inflicted on her as a battered wife. Can dreams be renewed and faith strengthened? Can they find joy and peace in God's love and in love for one another?

Tempered Fire (book 3 in Tempered Series)

The daughter of a wealthy rancher... A nobody from nowhere with nothing...Will their love survive?

Amber Harris is a good girl on the brink of womanhood. Stanley Morrison is a young man at the start of his life. For each other, they have always felt the fireworks that two people in love should feel. But the questions about his past, his pride, and Amber's father might be the end of what could be a strong relationship. As the two try to protect their budding romance, some unlikely but powerful forces conspire to keep them apart. Will they survive the wishes of everyone around them with their relationship intact?

Tempered Joy (book 4 in Tempered series)

He's an 'all around' cowboy. She thinks rodeo cowboys have rocks for brains and a death wish for a soul.

All around rodeo cowboy and heir to the

Rockin' H Ranch, Ace Harris is determined not to fall in love. He's only loved one woman in his life, his mother, and no one can even come close to filling her boots.

Lexie Morgan thinks rodeo cowboys have rocks for brains and a death wish for a soul. A broken childhood and the death of her father and best friend leave her doubting and questioning God (despite her years of religious upbringing) and afraid of love. Can two young people who clash from the onset learn to trust in the healing power of God and find love and happiness amidst tragedy and grief?

Tempered Truth (book 5 in the Tempered Series)

Will the truth set them free, or will it destroy a lifelong friendship?

Fate declared them neighbors. Scandal insisted they were brothers. The fact that they looked enough alike to be twins only added fuel to the rumors flying about their parentage.

For fifty-plus years Craig Harris and Scott Hensley have enjoyed a bond nothing can sever.

Not the insinuations that they share the same father.

Not the years of strife and grief and heartache.

Not even death.

Will the truth set them free, or will it destroy the friendship that has lasted a lifetime?

Tempered Journey

She's second-guessing her life choices. He's been widowed for over a decade. Will a case of mistaken identity bring two lonely souls together?

As a Registered Nurse and Energy Medicine Practitioner, Pat Greene has spent her entire life in service to others. But when her BFF finds true love for the second time, she finds herself surprisingly envious. Has her call to service—which she will never regret—somehow caused her to miss out on something special? The loneliness she's kept at bay gnaws at her heart. While in Bandera, Texas she has a chance encounter with the one man she's ever truly loved and is shocked to then discover he's **not** the man she thought he was.

The ache of loss still haunts Craig Harris a decade after his wife's death. Has his loyalty to her memory closed off his heart? Is he bound to an existence without the soul-deep joy he knows a woman's love can bring? Then he meets Pat Greene. Unprepared, he is bowled over by an instant, powerful spark of attraction—the kind he hasn't allowed himself to feel for years.

There's no mistaking the allure the

handsome cowboy holds for Pat, but the idea of giving up a lifetime of missionary work sets off a firestorm of doubt and indecision. Besides, Craig has children, grandchildren, and extended family members to think about.

The fact she mistakes him for his brother, with whom she had a brief relationship decades ago, tempers the initial magnetism that draws Craig toward Pat, but the more they get to know one another, the more he wants her in his life.

Will love be enough to tame the wanderlust in her soul and open his heart to the possibilities a future together might hold?

Tempered Journey is a later-in-life romance that shows the power of love to heal the loneliest of hearts. This novel brings together characters from the *Tempered* series and *My Heart Weeps*. We catch up with Melena and Garrett as well as Mike, Trina, and the rest of the Harris/Hensley clan as we journey into love with Craig Harris and Pat Greene. Get your copy today and fall in love with these characters all over again.

Lori's Redemption

Can a notorious bad girl find redemption & win the cowboy preacher's heart?

Lori Strickland (introduced in *Tempered Fire*) has always been known as her father's "wild child" with no desire to change until she meets ex-bull-rider-turned-preacher, Rafe Judson. Her attempts to change her wanton ways come to naught until she realizes redemption only comes with true repentance. Can she find redemption and win the heart of the cowboy preacher?

My Heart Weeps

When life takes everything, your world stops. Can a retreat heal the broken lives of two wounded souls?

Melena Rhyker's world shattered the day her husband died. Lost without the man of her dreams, she digs deep to find a path out of her sorrow. Discovering an artistic retreat, she vows to find a reason to carry on and focus her life in a new direction. Can she heal her own heart, and find her new beginning?

Garrett Saunders knows pain. He's spent most of his life hiding from his past. Regrets and lies haunt him, but he longs to leave them behind and embrace his true self. Will Melena's efforts to rebuild her life in the face of such grief encourage him to exorcise his own demons of guilt and shame?

Will two hurting people find peace, wholeness and perhaps love in the heart of Texas?

Get this second chance women's fiction novel today and see how love and faith conquers all.

Kyleigh's Cowboy

She's attempting to start a new life. He's roamed for more than a decade. Can they let go of the past and grab hold of the future?

Seven years after the death of her husband, Kyleigh Winters turned their old vacation home into a brand new guest ranch. Not willing to join the ranks of lonely women trolling the bars or online in search of a man, Kyleigh is sure if God wishes her to have another husband, He'll send the perfect someone in His own time. But will she be open to the possibility of new love when He does?

Searching for a place that calls to his soul, Lance Stevens has been a roaming cowboy for ten years since retiring from the Marines. He finds that sanctuary the moment he drives through the Silver Star's gate and meeting the lovely owner speaks to more than his soul. Will he open to the healing power of love?

Get Pamela Thibodeaux's second chance romance novella today and see how love and faith conquers all.

Keri's Christmas Wish

Controversy and Inconsistencies are thieves of holiday joy for Keri... Is there any hope for a happy holiday season?

For as long as she can remember, Keri Jackson has despised the hype and commercialism around Christmas—especially with the controversy over the time of Jesus' birth. Will she get her wish and be free of the angst to truly enjoy Christmas this year?

Jeremy Hinton thinks Keri is a highly intelligent, deeply emotional, and intensely complex woman and he's as fascinated by her aversion to Christmas as he is of the woman herself. A devout Christian at heart, he's studied all of the world's religions and homeopathic healing modalities. But when a rare bacterial infection threatens her life, will all of his faith and training be for naught?

Fans of near death experiences will enjoy this woman's mystical journey into spiritual Truth.

Circles of Fate

When two souls are torn apart by duty, can the hand of God bring them back to a happily ever after?

Late Vietnam War era. Strapped for cash,

Todd Jameson flirts with disaster. Caught robbing a liquor store to pay for his dad's funeral and given the choice of jail or signing up for the military, he picks the best of two bad options and joins the army. But just as his fresh start reconnects him with a sense of honor and the friendship of a gracious woman, he's deployed overseas into an unknown destiny.

Sixteen-year-old Shaunna Chatman devotes every breath to caring for her sick mother. Working in a diner to make ends meet, the last thing on her agenda is to fall for a young soldier about to be sent into battle. But when he encourages her not to wait, she reluctantly moves on to wed another who's there to pick up the pieces after she buries her beloved mom.

Thrown into a whirlwind of circumstance, Todd flows in and out of the courageous girl's narrative wondering if their stories will ever fully entwine. And though Shaunna's journey grants her a child even as personal tragedy strikes, her thoughts often turn to the boy who still fills her heart.

Will their paths merge once more to bask in the glory of His love?

Circles of Fate is a deeply woven inspirational women's fiction novel. If you like believable heroes, roads to enlightenment, and tales of inner strength, then you'll adore Pamela

S Thibodeaux's romantic saga.

Buy *Circles of Fate* to walk in the light today!

The Visionary

Will the ugly secret haunting the twins keep them from finding true love?

While most visionaries see into the future, Taylor sees the past. but only as it pertains to her work. Hailed by her peers as "a visionary with an instinct for beauty and an eye for the unique" Taylor is undoubtedly a brilliant architect and gifted designer. But she and twin brother Trevor share more than a successful business. The two share a childhood wrought with lies and deceit and the kind of abuse that's disturbingly prevalent in today's society.

Can the love of God and the awesome healing power of His grace and mercy free the twins from their past and open their hearts to the good plan and the future He has for their lives?

Love is a Rose (devotional)

Can God use a secular song to speak to someone and touch their heart?

Music is the magical entry into the spirit world, the golden gate into the Kingdom of God. But we mustn't be of the mindset that God only uses Christian music to reach out and touch our mind, heart, and spirit. God uses any and *every* means available to speak to His children.

Our job is to be open and receptive.

In this devotional, Pamela S Thibodeaux shares how God opened her spirit to a deeper understanding of the abundance of His grace and mercy through the words of the song, The Rose sung by Country & Western artist Conway Twitty.

Pamela offers Seeds to Ponder and a prayer as she parallels the love of God and the Christian life to each verse of the song.

Love's Overcoming Power eBook

Temptation, Abuse, Grief, and Doubt are plagues common to women all over the world. In John, 16 Jesus said.... In the world you will have tribulation but be of good cheer, for I have overcome the world.

In this Women's Fiction collection comprised of three full-length novels and one novella, Pamela S Thibodeaux shares stories that exemplify the power of God's love to overcome whatever situations life throws at you.

Includes: ***The Visionary, Circles of Fate, My Heart Weeps*** and ***Keri's Christmas Wish.***

Praise for Pamela S. Thibodeaux

*"**Kyleigh's Cowboy** was so beautifully written, that it literally made me cry. The hero and heroine were sympathetic yet flawed and I fell instantly in love with them. Wonderful Christian Cowboy Romance!"* ~ Amazon Reviewer T.P. Warren

"Pamela Thibodeaux uses her masterful story writing art to create a powerful story of how God heals a woman's heart —broken by grief— through recovery, love and triumph." ~ CBA Best-Selling Author DiAnn Mills on **My Heart Weeps**.

"Loved this book. Wish everyone could read this. Definitely puts all holidays in perspective. If we remember the reason for the holidays then we must put God first... Always. I will certainly recommend this book. Great stuff keep up the great writing." ~ (Amazon) Review of **Keri's Christmas Wish** by Reba

"Oh, the passion, faith and just LIFE that flows through this book... Powerful writing indeed!" ~ Review of **Circles of Fate** by Deena Peterson, Book Reviewer @ A Peek at my Bookshelf and Just One More

Once again.....Thank You...

I pray you are as blessed as I am by your purchase of this book. If you enjoy *A Hint of Romance,* please write a positive review, and post it at online retailers and websites where readers gather and/or your social media platforms (FaceBook, Good Reads, BookBub, Twitter, etc).

If you haven't already, sign up to receive my *Newsletter* and get a FREE short story.

Temperance
Publishing

9798989565023